"Dylan, I with anyone in over nine *months,"*

Lucy said.

Maybe, if he tried very hard, he could resist his own urges. But Dylan *couldn't* resist her. Hadn't the strength to turn his back on what she was offering him so willingly, not when every fiber of his body wanted her.

Not when *he* wanted her.

Ever since he'd walked out on her, he'd felt as if half his soul were missing. A soul he'd only found the very first time he made love with her. When she had shown him that making love was more than a matter of body coming to body. She'd shown him that there were souls involved, and feelings that transcended the physical.

"Are you sure?" he asked.

Rising on her toes, her lips a scant breath away from his, she whispered, "Very sure."

The last thread of his fraying resistance gave way....

Dear Reader,

As you have no doubt noticed, this year marks Silhouette Books' 20th anniversary, and for the next three months the spotlight shines on Intimate Moments, so we've packed our schedule with irresistible temptations.

First off, I'm proud to announce that this month marks the beginning of A YEAR OF LOVING DANGEROUSLY, a twelve-book continuity series written by eleven of your favorite authors. Sharon Sala, a bestselling, award-winning, absolutely incredible writer, launches things with *Mission: Irresistible,* and next year she will also write the final book in the continuity. Picture a top secret agency, headed by a man no one sees. Now picture a traitor infiltrating security, chased by a dozen (or more!) of the agency's best operatives. The trail crisscrosses the globe, and passion is a big part of the picture, until the final scene is played out and the final romance reaches its happy conclusion. Every book in A YEAR OF LOVING DANGEROUSLY features a self-contained romance, along with a piece of the ongoing puzzle, and enough excitement and suspense to fuel your imagination for the entire year. Don't miss a single monthly installment!

This month also features new books from top authors such as Beverly Barton, who continues THE PROTECTORS, and Marie Ferrarella, who revisits THE BABY OF THE MONTH CLUB. And in future months look for *New York Times* bestselling author Linda Howard, with *A Game of Chance* (yes, it's Chance Mackenzie's story at long last), and a special in-line two-in-one collection by Maggie Shayne and Marilyn Pappano, called *Who Do You Love?* All that and more of A YEAR OF LOVING DANGEROUSLY, as well as new books from the authors who've made Intimate Moments *the* place to come for a mix of excitement and romance no reader can resist. Enjoy!

Leslie J. Wainger
Executive Senior Editor

Please address questions and book requests to:
Silhouette Reader Service
U.S.: 3010 Walden Ave., P.O. Box 1325, Buffalo, NY 14269
Canadian: P.O. Box 609, Fort Erie, Ont. L2A 5X3

MARIE FERRARELLA

THE ONCE AND FUTURE FATHER

Published by Silhouette Books

America's Publisher of Contemporary Romance

To Tiffany Hsiang,
For all the wonderful things you are,
and
all the wonderful things you will be

SILHOUETTE BOOKS

ISBN 0-373-27087-9

THE ONCE AND FUTURE FATHER

Visit Silhouette at www.eHarlequin.com

Printed in U.S.A.

IT'S OUR 20th ANNIVERSARY!
We'll be celebrating all year,
Continuing with these fabulous titles,
On sale in July 2000.

Intimate Moments

#1015 Egan Cassidy's Kid
Beverly Barton

#1016 Mission: Irresistible
Sharon Sala

#1017 The Once and Future Father
Marie Ferrarella

#1018 Imminent Danger
Carla Cassidy

#1019 The Detective's Undoing
Jill Shalvis

#1020 Who's Been Sleeping in Her Bed?
Pamela Dalton

Special Edition

#1333 The Pint-Sized Secret
Sherryl Woods

#1334 Man of Passion
Lindsay McKenna

 50th book

#1335 Whose Baby Is This?
Patricia Thayer

#1336 Married to a Stranger
Allison Leigh

#1337 Doctor and the Debutante
Pat Warren

#1338 Maternal Instincts
Beth Henderson

Desire

 MAN OF THE MONTH

#1303 Bachelor Doctor
Barbara Boswell

 body & soul

#1304 Midnight Fantasy
Ann Major

#1305 Wife for Hire
Amy J. Fetzer

 TEXAS GROOMS

#1306 Ride a Wild Heart
Peggy Moreland

#1307 Blood Brothers
Anne McAllister & Lucy Gordon

#1308 Cowboy for Keeps
Kristi Gold

Romance

AN OLDER MAN

#1456 Falling for Grace
Stella Bagwell

 The Circle K Sisters

#1457 The Borrowed Groom
Judy Christenberry

#1458 Denim & Diamond
Moyra Tarling

 THE CARRAMER CROWN

#1459 The Monarch's Son
Valerie Parv

 BRIDAL FEVER!

#1460 Jodie's Mail-Order Man
Julianna Morris

#1461 Lassoed!
Martha Shields

Chapter 1

"Some guys just don't have any luck, you know what I mean?"

The burly police detective abruptly stopped talking, a coughing fit seizing him. "I mean, this is supposed to be one of the safest cities of our size in the country, and this poor jerk gets wasted right here, in beautiful downtown Bedford."

Separated by a four-foot-high partition, Dylan McMorrow could hear the crinkle of cellophane. Alexander, the man who was talking, was dipping into his supply of hard candy. Cellophane wrappers marked his trail in the precinct wherever he went.

"Maybe not," Hathaway, Alexander's partner, speculated. "The body was moved, remember?"

"Yeah, but it was found here, so that puts it in our jurisdiction." The sound of drawers being opened and closed in quick succession floated over the partition. Alexander was always looking for something to write on. From the sound of it, he hadn't found it. Dylan concentrated on shutting the distraction out. He had an overdue expense report to get out. "This is my first homicide. You ever handle one before?" Alexander asked Hathaway.

The other man's laugh was tinged in disbelief. "I'm from L.A., remember?"

"Sorry." Alexander shoved another drawer closed. "Well, at least we've got an ID on him. Ritchie Alvarez."

Dylan's long fingers froze on the keyboard. The squad room, like everything else within the Bedford Police Department's three-story, modern building, was the last word in precision, neatness and state-of-the-art equipment. There were computers on every detective's desk rather than a faltering, centrally located electric typewriter the way there had been at his last precinct.

But Dylan wasn't thinking of his last precinct, or even what had brought him back here to Bedford, California, after a requested six-month loan-out.

He was thinking of a woman. A golden-skinned woman with hair the color of a sensual midnight sky, honey on her lips and laughter in her dark eyes.

Lucy.

He felt his gut tightening the way it always did when he thought of her. Dylan reminded himself to breathe. Slowly.

Alvarez was a common-enough name among those with even a marginal claim to a Spanish heritage. And as for Ritchie...

How many Ritchie Alvarezes were there in a city the size of Bedford?

Getting to his feet, Dylan looked over the partition at the two other detectives. "How do you know his name?" he asked.

Detective Marcus Alexander was startled by Dylan's question and almost dropped his coffee mug. He steadied it at the last moment, glaring at Dylan.

"Jeez, McMorrow, don't you know better than to sneak up on a man like that?"

There was no expression on Dylan's face. There usually wasn't. It made it harder for people to second-guess him that way.

"I didn't sneak. You were standing next to my cubicle. Talking rather loudly." Dylan's voice, like his manner, was low, with an edge to it that warned the listener not to test him. "How do you know his name?" he asked again.

Reaching into his pocket, Alexander took out a clear plastic pouch. Inside was a single sheet of wrinkled paper.

"It's on this bank statement. We found it crumpled up in his inside pocket." Alexander held the pouch out for Dylan's examination. "Killer must have missed it when he took the victim's wallet."

The other detective, Mick Hathaway, turned around the chair he was sitting in and looked up at Dylan, curious. "Why? You know him?"

Dylan regarded the bank statement. It was to notify one Ritchie Alvarez that his checking account was overdrawn. Again. That was Ritchie to a *T,* Dylan thought. He gave the evidence back to Alexander. "Might." His eyes shifted to Hathaway, the more experienced of the two. "You have the crime scene shots on you?"

"Right here." Brushing his jacket aside, Hathaway reached into his inside pocket. One by one he lay down on the desk the four instant photographs taken of the victim. Hathaway slanted a glance in Dylan's direction.

"Damn," Dylan commented.

"Then you know him?" Hathaway asked.

Dylan dragged his hand through his unruly black hair, wishing he'd been wrong. "Yeah, I know him. Knew him. The name's right."

"Know if he has a next of kin?" Hathaway questioned.

Dylan blew out a breath, and tried to blow back memories he didn't want crowding him. It didn't work. "A sister. Last I remember, he was staying at her place. Always did when he was down on his luck."

Hathaway shook his head. "Looks like he got even more down."

"Looks like." *Dammit, Ritchie, why weren't you more careful with your life?* Dylan wondered.

Disgusted at the waste, bright shining moments shimmering in his mind's eye, Dylan let the photograph drop back amid the others. He fought a brief tug-of-war between his conscience and his need for self-preservation. It wasn't much of a contest.

He looked at Alexander. "Look, I know it's your case, and I'm not trying to horn in here, but if you need someone to break it to his sister—"

Alexander looked relieved beyond words. "Hey, be my guest. I wouldn't know where to begin." Belatedly, he looked at Hathaway. "Okay with you?"

Collecting the photographs, Hathaway carefully

tucked them away again. "More than okay. If you want to take down her statement—"

Dylan nodded. Lucy wouldn't have had anything to do with whatever it was that had brought Ritchie to this miserable juncture. But to say so might arouse further curiosity, and the two other men were already looking at him as if he'd just bared his soul to them. Though partnered, Dylan kept to himself most of the time, and he made a point of never saying any more than he had to. It gave the other guy too much ammunition that way.

He glanced at his watch, but he knew what time it was even without checking. He was on his own time right now. He'd come in early to finish up the expense report, but that would have to wait until he got off later. "I'm not due for my shift until another couple of hours. The sister's statement probably won't be much to take down."

As Dylan began to leave, Hathaway rose to block his path. Dylan saw the questions beginning to form in the other detective's eyes. Maybe Dylan shouldn't have said anything, but to leave this kind of news for a stranger to break to Lucy just didn't seem right.

"Where do you know him from?" Hathaway asked.

Dylan sidestepped the older man. "We shared a couple of classes." It was far more than that, but he didn't want to get into it. Into the friendship they had enjoyed and what had come after.

Surprised, Alexander called after him. "You mean he's from around here?"

"Born and raised" was all Dylan said as he walked out the door.

* * *

He knew the way to Lucy's place by heart.

Lucy would probably say he didn't have a heart. Not that he could blame her. But he'd done what he'd done more for her than for him. Someday, she'd appreciate that.

Or not, he amended. Eventually, it would all be one and the same. Time would see to that. Maybe it already had, he mused. Over the last nine months, he'd purposely lost track of her, purposely stayed away from all the old haunts where he thought he might run into her.

The only place he couldn't escape her was in his mind. But he would. Eventually.

He'd known Ritchie a number of years before he ever met the sister that Ritchie was so fond of. There had been something different about Lucy from the first moment Dylan saw her, but he'd tried not to notice, tried not to pay any more attention to her than he would any one of a number of beautiful women who passed through his life. But she'd been more, right from the start. And for a while, for eight precious months, he'd deluded himself that he could have a normal life, the kind he'd only heard about.

Part of him figured he had to be crazy, seeking Lucy out after nine months of a self-imposed moratorium. Dylan knew he wasn't in a place where he could say he was over her. He doubted that he would ever really be over Lucinda Alvarez, but at least it had gotten to the point where she didn't start and end each day, lingering in the perimeter of his thoughts like the deep scent of roses. He'd managed to get through whole chunks of the day without so much as thinking of her.

Or what they could have had.

If he had been someone else.

But another part of him knew he had to do this. Owed it to her for the history they had. She didn't deserve to hear about Ritchie from either Alexander or Hathaway, good men both, but not exactly sensitive when it came to something like this.

Yeah, right, like he was Mr. Sensitivity, he silently mocked himself as he waited for the traffic light to change.

She didn't deserve to hear the words at all, he thought impatiently, but that was life and he hadn't written it. All he could do was try to change some of the footnotes.

Dylan realized that he was gripping the steering wheel as if he were engaged in a life-and-death struggle and loosened his fingers. He wished he could change this particular footnote. Ritchie had been a good guy. Just incredibly unlucky.

Weren't they all? he thought.

"I'm sorry, Lucy," he whispered under his breath as he turned down her street and saw the neat dove-gray-and-blue-trimmed stucco house.

So where was Ritchie, already?

Impatient, Lucy Alvarez glanced at her wristwatch, the one with the band she had yet to replace. But she was still stupidly sentimental about the watch. It had been a gift. The first gift. When there had been promise in the air.

She sighed, squelching the temptation to look out

the window again. It wouldn't make her brother appear any faster.

Ritchie probably forgot, she thought. She'd asked him to take her to the doctor just this one time, because it was so hard for her to find a comfortable position behind the steering wheel these last few weeks. Two weeks overdue, she was painfully aware of every second that went by beyond her delivery date.

He'd promised to be here.

But Ritchie's promises were always the same—made quickly, with enthusiasm, and then forgotten. Not from any malice, but just because that was Ritchie. He had the attention span of a gnat.

Lucy nibbled on her lower lip, debating whether or not to call a cab. She didn't want to be late for her appointment.

However, by the time the cab finally arrived, she would probably miss it altogether.

Still, if he wasn't here... Lucy picked up the receiver and began to dial.

The sound of the doorbell ringing had her hanging up the telephone. Ritchie was here. Finally. The fact that he was ringing the doorbell instead of unlocking the door himself didn't strike her as particularly odd. He'd probably forgotten his key. Ritchie would've misplaced his head if it hadn't been attached.

Someday, he was going to drive whatever poor woman he made his wife crazy. Until then, he was hers to look after. Moving awkwardly, Lucy made her way to the front door. The doorbell rang once more.

''What's the matter, Ritchie, lose your key again, not to mention your watch? You're late—''

Flipping open the lock, Lucy began to launch into a lecture she knew would do no more good than any of the others she'd given him over the course of the last few years. Her tolerant smile faded as she abruptly stopped and stared at the man standing in her doorway. Her heart leaped up, and then down, lodging itself somewhere, uncomfortably, halfway in between.

For just the briefest of seconds, she thought she was hallucinating.

But she was wide awake and he was here, filling out her doorway with his dark good looks the way he had once filled out her entire life.

Dylan.

Funny how much smarter you can become in just nine months.

Her hand on the door, she kept it where it was, half opened, half closed, a barrier to keep him out. The way he had kept her out.

Pressing her lips together, she raised herself on her toes to look over his shoulder, hoping to see the broken-down car her brother drove coming up the street. But it wasn't in sight.

Her eyes narrowed as she looked at Dylan. ''What are you doing here? If you're here to see Ritchie, he's not home. I'm waiting for him myself.''

Dylan's mind went blank as he stared at her. At the one woman who had managed to somehow get past his defenses.

She was pregnant.

Not huge, the way Hathaway's wife had been just

before she'd given birth to their twins, but Lucy was pregnant, carrying a life inside of her, there was no missing that.

She'd said she'd love him, no matter what.

This, he guessed, was "what."

A wild, hot jealousy rippled through Dylan, born years before he had been, a seed his father had passed down to him and his father before him. For one horrid second, it felt as if that jealousy, that seed, had taken him over, changing the very world that was around him, sending it into tints of red and closing off his air.

Dylan struggled to banish the feeling the way he'd banished his father from his life.

This wasn't why he was here. Lucy's life was her own. He'd given it back to her when he'd withdrawn from it, leaving her alone.

Whose baby was it?

The question throbbed through his brain like a bad migraine.

"Did you hear me?" Lucy demanded, her voice rising. "I said Ritchie's not home. He's working. I'll tell him you stopped by."

Because it hurt just to look at Dylan, she began to close the door. But his hand went out, stopping her. She hadn't the strength to oppose it.

"What?" she demanded, trying to hang on to her temper, on to the angry tears that had suddenly sprung up inside of her, demanding a release. Why was he back now, after all this time? She was just getting her life back in order. She didn't need this. And why was he looking at her like that?

"This is about Ritchie," Dylan said.

She turned pale right before his eyes, holding the

door now not so much to block him as for support, to keep from sinking down like a balloon that had suddenly lost all its air. His hand went out to steady her, but she ignored it, stiffening with her last available ounce of dignity. The message was clear. She didn't need him to touch her.

Lucy felt herself getting light-headed. "What about Ritchie?" she asked, holding on to the door for support.

"Lucy, let's go inside."

She didn't budge. She didn't have the strength to budge. Ritchie was her older brother, but she had always felt responsible for him. Especially after their parents had died in a train derailment the summer she turned eighteen. Ritchie was the one who could laugh, who could see the bright side of everything even when the chips were down. She was the strength that helped them go on.

She didn't feel very strong now.

Summoning what reserves she had left, Lucy glared at Dylan. Why was he playing these games with her? Why did he have to be the one to come and tell her whatever it was he had to say?

She clenched her teeth together and repeated. "What about Ritchie?"

Dylan didn't want to tell her this way. Not on the steps of the house where he had once held her in his arms, breathing in her scent and contemplating things he had no right to contemplate. But Lucy was making no move to let him in, standing instead like some steadfast soldier guarding the borders of her small country, refusing him access.

He tried not to think of a time when things had been different.

Dylan looked at her face. She was fiercely trying to protect herself against what she probably knew was coming. He had no idea how to couch this, how to make something that was so utterly devastating a little less so.

Without a choice, Dylan gave her the news straight and braced himself for the consequences.

"Ritchie's dead, Lucy."

Lucy's breath caught. She looked into Dylan's eyes and knew he was telling her the truth. She knew even when she wanted to scream at him that he was lying, that he was playing some sort of horrible trick on her, the way he had when he made her believe he loved her. He had never said the words, but there had been feelings between them then, feelings she would have gone to her grave swearing were true.

Except that they weren't. At least, not for him.

But now it was Ritchie who was going to his grave.

Everything around her began to merge into one color, one huge mass. And then the world began to swim and swirl.

"No," she mouthed just before everything went black and swallowed her up.

Dylan realized a heartbeat before it happened that she was going to faint. The golden hue of her skin had gone whiter than the snow on the mountain where they had once gone skiing. It was almost translucent.

Dylan reached her side just in time.

The swell that was her unborn child came between them. He felt something move, something kick just as he tried to gather her in his arms. The kick caught him by surprise and he almost dropped her to the floor. The sudden jolt when he caught her seemed to travel through the length of her. Dylan swallowed a curse.

He felt the baby kick again. Amid his concern, jealousy threatened to take control of him.

She'd gone on to love someone else while he had suffered in his own private hell.

A hell, a voice deep inside him whispered, of his own making, not hers.

But it had been the only choice.

He wouldn't allow himself to feel anything now. It wasn't any more right now than it had been then.

As gently as possible, Dylan picked her up in his arms. Shouldering his way into the living room, he placed Lucy down on the sofa. Probably the bedroom would have been a better choice, but he couldn't bring himself to go there.

Unbuttoning the three tiny buttons at her throat, he tried to remember what a man did in a case like this. And tried not to think about the last time he'd undressed her.

He realized that his hand was shaking slightly.

Dammit, whatever might have been between them was over now. She was carrying somebody else's baby. He glanced at her left hand. There was no ring on her third finger, but that meant nothing. She could have taken the ring off because her hand had gotten swollen.

He should have left this to Hathaway and Alexander. At least if he had, he wouldn't have found out that Lucy was pregnant.

Cursing himself for coming and Ritchie for being stupid enough to get himself killed in the first place,

Dylan hurried into the kitchen to look for something to use as a compress. He found a single kitchen towel neatly folded on a rack. He'd once marveled how she managed to keep everything so neat, given Ritchie's penchant for creating havoc wherever he went. Grabbing the kitchen towel from the rack, he held it under running water.

Wringing the towel out, he looked around the kitchen. A sense of nostalgia permeated. As with the living room, nothing had changed in here.

Only she had.

Not his concern, he told himself tersely.

The wet towel fell from his fingers when he heard the scream. Racing back, he found her trying to sit up. There was pain etched into the planes of her face. Lucy was digging her nails into the upper portion of the sofa, whether to try to drag herself up or to try to get away from pain, he didn't know.

"What's the matter?" The question came out far more sharply than he'd intended.

"The baby." Trying to catch her breath, Lucy pressed the flat of her hand against her stomach. Her eyes were huge when she raised them to his face. "Dylan, the baby's coming."

Chapter 2

Her words cut through Dylan like a sharp razor. An edgy sense of panic hovered over him. "Are you sure? You just fainted, maybe—"

"There's no 'maybe' about it—the baby is coming." Her eyes widened as another thrust of pain, on the heels of the last, began burrowing to the surface. "Now."

"Hang on," he cautioned. Dylan could feel his own heart rate accelerating. Pulling out his cell phone, he dialed the precinct's dispatch. "This is Detective McMorrow. I need an ambulance ASAP." He gave the woman on the other end Lucy's address, then flipped the phone shut. "They'll be here in ten minutes."

Lucy's breaths came in snatches, like someone, already exhausted, climbing up the side of a steep mountain. The thick black hair that had been so seductively sensuous to touch was plastered against her face. Dylan could see that she was fighting pain with every fiber of her being.

There was no use trying to distance himself from the scene. It got to him. Dylan couldn't stand seeing her like this.

Her eyes rose to his for a single moment before she shut them again. "I don't think that's going to be fast enough."

All the labor horror stories that Dylan vaguely recalled hearing came back to him now. Wasn't the process supposed to go on for interminable hours? "You're kidding, right?"

Unable to answer, Lucy moved her head from side to side, her teeth sinking into her lower lip so hard he was afraid she was going to bite straight through it. Momentarily at a loss, Dylan took her hand and felt his fingers immediately caught up in a viselike grip. The strength of it took him by surprise.

"No," she said, finally managing to breathe, "I'm not. I can feel the pressure...it's like...I'm being...pulled apart...like a giant...*wishbone.*" Lucy shrieked the last part of the word as a salvo of pain thundered through her. Her eyes were wide as she looked at him.

He saw the fear and forgot his own. He forced himself to stop thinking of her as Lucy and start thinking of her as a woman who needed his help. After all, he was a cop and that was what he did, he helped people in need. He couldn't let it get any more complicated than that.

But it was, a voice whispered inside of him. No matter how hard he tried to block out the truth, this was still Lucy. And he was going to have to help her give birth to another man's child.

The realization hit hard into his soul.

With fingers that were in danger of going numb, he managed to squeeze her hand, reassuring her the only way he knew how. Silently.

"Okay, Lucy, if he's going to come now, let's get this going."

Dylan thought a minute, trying to remember a class he'd been forced to take in his earlier days as a policeman. The particulars he needed now were obscure. All he could recall was thinking that he hoped he'd never have to face the situation himself. And now here he was.

Yes, here he was, and at the moment, he was all that Lucy had to cling to. It was probably his fault that she'd gone into labor in the first place. Maybe if he'd had a better way of telling her...

Water under the bridge, Dylan admonished himself. Speculation wasn't going to change what was happening now. And that was what he had to deal with.

"I don't think...I...have a choice." Without consciously meaning to, she dug her fingernails into his flesh as he tried to disengage his hand from hers. Another contraction had seized her, holding her prisoner. Torturing her.

Freeing himself as gently as he could, he turned her face so that she was forced to look at him. He willed his strength into her.

"Breathe, Lucy, breathe. Small, shallow breaths. Concentrate on breathing."

"I can't."

His voice was stern. "Yes, you can."

It wasn't encouragement as much as an order. That was what she needed right now, someone strong to help her find her way. He stowed away any stray feelings that might have still been lingering and galvanized his resolve.

Mechanically, Dylan lifted the hem of her dress and pushed it up to her waist, then as quickly as possible, he removed her underwear. He saw her body stiffen, not from his touch, but because the next contraction had begun on the perimeter of the one that was only now releasing her. She writhed in agony, holding her breath, as if that could somehow make it go away.

"Breathe, dammit!" he ordered. Catching her chin in his hands, he forced her to look at him again. "Like this." His eyes holding hers, he took in a long breath and released it in short pants. "Okay?"

Anger, anchorless and sharp, raged through her. At him, at Ritchie, at the pain. But there was no outlet and she was not master of her soul right now. The pain saw to that.

Lucy did as she was told, holding on to Dylan's order as if it were a lifeline, a single thing to focus that would lead her out of this ring of fire she found herself in. She had a life inside of her. A life that was struggling to be brought into this world, and she owed it to her child to help in any way she could.

And Dylan would help both of them. For this one thing, she could count on him.

Closing her eyes, listening to the sound of Dylan's voice echoing in her head, she began to push.

She'd stopped breathing. His eyes darted back up

to her face. It was contorted. Dylan realized that she was pushing. Damn it, where the hell were the paramedics? Why weren't they here yet?

"Okay, you're doing fine, just fine," Dylan said. "I can see it, Lucy. I can see the top of the baby's head."

Dylan's voice and the words he said barely registered inside the haze of pain surrounding her. And then they seemed to take on a breadth, a thickness of their own. The baby. Her baby. It was almost here. Hunching her shoulders forward, she fought off the waves of exhaustion that had come from the dark to encircle her and forced herself to push again. Harder this time. Longer. Until finally, too drained to continue, she fell back against the sofa cushion, gasping for air.

"Don't stop now," he ordered.

"Dylan, I'm so tired...."

"He can't do it alone, and he wants to be here now." Dylan moved behind Lucy, gathering together the decorative pillows she'd scattered around and shoving them under her shoulders to help prop her up. "Finally know what it means to want to be in two places at once," she heard him mutter under his breath. She opened her eyes to look at him and saw him smiling encouragingly at her. Then he slid back to take up the position where he'd been.

"Okay, on the count of three, I want you to push again. Ready?"

"No." The response was more of a sob than a word.

He raised his eyes to hers and the short, abrupt order on his lips softened in the face of the pain he saw. Damn, but she could still get to him like nothing and no one else ever had.

"Yes," he told her softly, "you are. Okay now, one, two, three. Push!" He felt every fiber of his own body tightening in concentration as he gave her the order.

Lucy pushed. Pushed so hard she felt as if she had ejected every fiber of her body, turning it completely inside out. Pushed so hard she thought she was going to faint again as a border of blackness began leeching into the feverish red haze that was engulfing her.

The final push came with a whining scream.

Falling back, she barely had enough strength left to gulp in air. Lucy heard a small, piercing cry. Was that coming from her? Or somewhere else?

But her own lips were closed now and the tiny, reedy wail persisted. Her lashes felt damp as she forced her eyes open. She could barely focus on Dylan. He was holding something in his arms.

Her baby.

She tried to wet her dry lips with the tip of her tongue, barely able to move it. "Is he…is he…all right?"

When Dylan didn't answer, a sliver of panic wedged itself in her breast, going straight for her heart like a sharp dagger. With her last ounce of strength, she raised herself up on her elbows.

"Dylan?"

He couldn't ever remember feeling like this before. Awed, overwhelmed with something very odd squeezing at his heart. And all because of the tiny life he held in his hands.

As if it had been stored on a delayed relay system, Lucy's tone played itself back to him. He raised his eyes to hers. A hint of a smile tugged on his lips, as if afraid to intrude on a moment this sacred.

''He's a she.'' His mouth curved a little more. ''Your son is a daughter—and she's more than all right. She's beautiful.''

Deprived of the warm shelter that had been hers only moments earlier, the infant began to squirm and cry. The thick thatch of black hair on her head was matted and plastered to her, and when she opened her eyes, they were the most incredible shade of blue Dylan had ever seen. He raised his eyes to look at Lucy.

''Are you able to hold her?''

''Try and stop me,'' Lucy said. Her heart was still racing, fueled by what she'd just been through and the exhilaration she felt now, seeing her daughter in Dylan's arms. Weak, she still managed to hold out her own arms to him.

Very gently, Dylan placed the tiny being against Lucy's breast. The same bittersweet feeling flittered over him. He didn't know what to make of it, what to call it, or how to store it. So he did the only thing he could, he locked it away in its entirety.

''She's messy,'' he murmured.

Exhausted as she was, Lucy could feel her heart constricting. She'd never known she could feel this much love at one time.

''She'll clean up,'' Lucy whispered. In awe of the tiny being she held, Lucy lightly passed her hand over the dark little head.

Watching, Dylan roused himself. It wasn't over yet. He still needed to cut the umbilical cord. He hurried to the kitchen for a knife and was halfway back before he stopped. The knife needed to be sterilized.

But when he turned toward the stove, intending to hold the blade over one of the burner flames, he saw only electrical coils. There were no gas jets.

Damn. His hands bloodied, Dylan automatically felt in his pants pocket before he remembered. He didn't smoke anymore. He no longer had a reason to carry matches.

Frustrated, he looked around the kitchen. He didn't have time to go rifling through drawers and cabinets. "You have any matches?" he shouted.

"No, why?"

"Because I need to—"

Walking back into the living room, he stopped short when he saw a whiskey decanter on the small wet bar. He recognized it. He'd given Ritchie the decanter just before he'd left for good. It'd been to celebrate something, but he no longer remembered the occasion. The decanter was still half-full. Dylan snatched it up.

"Never mind, this'll do." He removed the top and poured some of the contents of the decanter over the blade, covering it liberally. Except for the baby breathing, there was no other sound in the room. He could feel Lucy's eyes on him, watching. "I have to cut the cord."

"I know." She pressed the baby closer to her, though she knew it wouldn't hurt the infant.

He looked so removed, so dispassionate as he severed the cord that connected her so literally to her baby. Had he felt the same way when he cut the cord that had existed between them? Had it taken just one swift motion and it was done?

Once she would have believed she'd meant more to him than that. Now she knew better.

"There." The cord cut, Dylan sat back on his heels and looked at them.

The baby, still bloody, was nestled against Lucy. She had ceased crying and was dozing against her mother. It took everything he had not to touch the infant again, not to run the tip of his finger along the dewy skin.

The moment, soft and tender, hung between them. Echoes of the past threatened to overtake him. Rising to his feet, Dylan backed away.

He nodded toward where he remembered the linen closet was. "I should get something to wrap her up in." He needed distance between them. Distance between the thoughts he was having.

The sound of someone knocking on the door penetrated. "I'll get that."

"Since you're up," she murmured weakly.

"Yeah." He turned on his heel, hurrying to the front door. Dylan felt ashamed for feeling relieved at the reprieve. But there was far too much going on inside of him to deal with right now.

He made it to the door in less than five strides and pulled it open. The ambulance attendants had arrived. "Took you long enough."

The two paramedics, both in their early twenties, exchanged glances. The blonder of the two pushed the gurney into the house. "Hey, we went through every red light from the station house to here."

The other paramedic looked Dylan over. There

was blood on his shirt and on one of his pants pockets. "What the hell happened to you, McMorrow?"

His adrenaline beginning to settle, he realized that he hadn't given any details when he'd called for the ambulance, only saying he needed one. The attendants hadn't known if they were coming to the site of a homicide or a heart attack.

He glanced down at his shirt. "I got this playing midwife. The lady couldn't wait for you two to get here."

Only a short distance away, Lucy heard him and something inside of her cringed. The lady. As if they didn't know each other. As if they hadn't held each other in their arms and made love until both of them could have sworn that the morning would come to find not a breath of life left between them.

Tears stung her eyes. She pressed her lips together, telling herself she was over him. What they had was in the past, long gone and buried. There was someone else who needed her now.

The younger of the two paramedics looked at Lucy as he lined up the cot beside the sofa. He gave her a warm smile.

"Looks like you did half our job for us, Detective." The paramedic glanced at Dylan. "Nice work."

Dylan made no comment, standing off to the side as the two paramedics quickly took vital signs from mother and daughter. It was only when Lucy's eyes sought him out that he moved from the sidelines. He'd had every intention of leaving, but there was something in her eyes that had him changing his mind.

"I'll follow you in the car."

The paramedic closest to Dylan spared him a glance once they had secured mother and child on the gurney. ''You might want to change that shirt first. Unless you want everyone to think you were in an accident.''

An accident.

It had been in an accident that he had allowed himself to feel something, to give way to a temporary lapse in judgment and actually believe that he could be like everyone else.

That he was free to love and feel like everyone else.

But he knew better.

''I'll change later,'' he muttered as he followed them out the front door.

Dylan pulled it shut behind him, making sure the lock was secure before he hurried to his car. It was only as he waited for the driver of the ambulance to start the vehicle that Dylan allowed himself to sag, resting his head against the steering wheel. It was the only outward sign of fatigue he allowed himself. And only for a moment. Anything more and his control could break.

He was too numb to think. He wouldn't have let himself think if he could. It was better that way.

Or so he told himself.

Since he knew the ambulance's destination, he actually made it to Harris Memorial's emergency room parking lot a hairbreadth behind the vehicle. He was out of his car and at the ambulance's back door just as the attendant was opening it. He helped the man lower the gurney, then took his position at its side as Lucy and her baby were guided through the electronic doors.

Dylan curbed the urge to take Lucy's hand, curbed the urge to touch her. The less contact he had with her, the better. There'd already been far more than he'd bargained on.

Then what was he doing here, trotting beside the gurney if he had no intention of getting any closer than he had? he demanded silently. He was supposed to be on duty, taking his turn at maintaining surveillance, not halfway across town on the ground floor of Bedford's most popular hospital.

What he was doing here, he told himself, was being a friend. To Ritchie if not to Lucy. And Ritchie's sister had been through a great deal. She'd had both death and life flung at her within the space of less than half an hour. Even if there had been no history between him and Lucy, if ever he saw a woman who looked like she needed a friend, it was her. Process of elimination made him the closest one she had around.

"I have a doctor here," he heard her saying weakly to the attendant walking just ahead of him beside the gurney. "Sheila Pollack."

Dylan was vaguely familiar with the name. He'd heard several of the men at the precinct mention the woman, saying their wives and girlfriends swore by her. He grasped at the tidbit, needing something to do, to make himself useful. Anything to keep him from coming face-to-face with the past and have to deal with it.

"I can have her paged," he told the paramedic. He turned to go to the registration desk.

"Don't bother, we'll call her office," an amiable,

matronly-looking nurse told Dylan as she came up to join the delegation around the gurney.

He fell back without a word, feeling useless.

"Don't go," Lucy called to him. "I want to talk to you. About Ritchie."

"It'll have to wait until we get you cleaned up, honey," the nurse told her. "My, but that is one beautiful baby. You do nice work." She glanced at Dylan. "Is this the baby's daddy?"

Lucy forced herself not to look in Dylan's direction. "No."

Dylan tried to grab at the excuse the nurse had inadvertently given him. It was a legitimate way out of this uncomfortable situation. And he did have to get to the stakeout.

But Lucy's eyes were imploring him to stay. The excuse died on his lips before he had a chance to say it. There was no way around it. They had unfinished business to tend to.

"I'll wait in the hall until you're ready," he called after her.

She raised her voice. They were almost around a corner. "Promise?"

"Promise."

Her voice lingered after she disappeared from view. "I'll hold you to that."

His lips curved before he could think better of it. "I know."

Chapter 3

Dylan straightened up slowly. His back had begun to ache, and it felt as if it was taking on the shape of the hospital wall he'd been leaning against. He'd been waiting out in the maternity ward corridor far longer than he figured he should have.

He glanced at his watch. It was time to go.

He'd put in another call to dispatch the moment Lucy's gurney had disappeared behind closed doors. This time he'd had them patch him through to Dave Watley, the man he'd been partnered with off and on over the years. The message was short, terse. He was going to be late. Watley had been surprised, but he'd hung up before the man could ask why.

Even as he'd rung off, Dylan had fought his own silent battle over the wisdom of hanging around outside Lucy's hospital room.

He had a job to do and it wasn't here.

Still, he hadn't given Lucy any sort of accounting about her brother. In his defense, there'd been next to no time. But that didn't change the fact that he owed it to her.

Frustrated, he shoved his hands into his pockets, purposely avoiding looking in the general direction of the nursery. He didn't need that sort of distraction right now.

And Lucy didn't need to listen to the grisly details about her brother's death right now, he thought. She certainly wasn't in any shape to answer questions. Though part of him wanted to get this all over with and put everything behind him so he could start fresh again, he knew it'd be better for both the department and Lucy if he came back later, when she was up to it.

Or maybe not at all. Maybe if someone else handled this, it'd be for the best all around.

"Excuse me?"

Having made up his mind, Dylan had turned toward the elevators and his escape route. The low voice, aimed in his direction, momentarily put his plans on hold. Dylan looked over his shoulder to see a refined, tall blonde comfortably attired in a white lab coat that partially covered a blue sundress. She was looking straight at him. "Are you Detective McMorrow?"

"Yes?"

The verification was tendered slowly, cautiously, telling Sheila Pollack that this man was more accustomed to receiving bad news than good. And that, police detective or not, the tall, rangy man before her was a private person. Not a bit like her Slade.

With a smile meant to put him at his ease, she offered him her hand.

"Hi, I'm Sheila Pollack, Lucy's doctor. She told me you delivered the baby." She smiled and offered Dylan her hand.

He shook her hand mechanically, surprised at the firmness of the woman's grip. "The baby more or less delivered herself. I was just there to catch her."

"That's not the way Lucy tells it." Her smile grew sunnier. "Nice job."

Dylan shrugged, accepting the compliment the way he accepted any compliment that came his way, offhandedly and with little attention. It was criticism that helped a man grow, not empty words. His father had beaten that one into him until he'd been able to defend himself.

He looked over the doctor's head toward the room where they had taken Lucy and her baby. "How she's doing?"

"Mother and daughter are fine, no small thanks to you. Right now, they're both asleep. I think the ordeal exhausted them." She studied him for a moment. "Lucky for Lucy that you were there."

"Yeah, lucky," he muttered more to himself than to the statuesque woman. She was looking at him as if she could read his mind. Annoyed with himself, he dismissed the thought as ridiculous. "Well, I'm on duty, Doctor. I'd better go."

Sheila nodded. She had other patients on the floor to look in on. And a roomful waiting for her back at her office. But because each of her patients was more than simply just that to her, she paused where she was for one more second.

"Want me to tell Lucy anything when she wakes

up?'' When he made no reply, she asked, "Will you be back to see her?''

Dylan thought it an odd question. For all she knew, he'd just been someone passing by at the right time, or the wrong time, depending on whose view you took. But, then, he amended, maybe Lucy had told her that they'd known each other once.

For the sake of brevity and to prevent any possibility of further discussion, he said, "Yeah, sure," and quickly walked away.

Sheila spared herself a moment to watch him go, aware that she had just been brushed off. Instinct told her that there was a great deal more going on here than was evident at first.

Turning away, she smiled to herself. He'd be back. Whether he realized it or not, he'd be back. She was willing to lay odds on it.

Detective Dave Watley glanced up from the video camera he was adjusting. It was perched on a tripod, its powerful telephoto lens aimed at the entrance of the restaurant five stories below and across the street. "What the hell kept you?" he asked Dylan when his partner entered the apartment.

Pulling up a folding chair to the partially curtained window with one hand, Dylan placed the paper tray with its two cups of coffee on the unsteady card table. Besides a beaten-up sofa that had been abandoned by the last tenant who lived in the apartment, the card table and two chairs represented the only furniture in the studio apartment. Watley had brought the table. He needed someplace to put the puzzles he was so fond of working on.

"I was detained." Dylan pried his own cup from the holder, leaving the one he'd picked up for Watley where it was.

Watley looked at him with good-natured disgust. "No kidding, Sherlock. I kind of figured that part out for myself. Detained how?"

As far as Watley knew, his rather closed-mouth partner had no personal life to speak of, no relatives he ever mentioned, and certainly no woman in his life. The man lived and breathed the job, which made him a good man to have watching your back, but not exactly the best to share a long stakeout with. And this one had all the signs of being a long one, even though it was just in its third day.

Because nothing else came to him and he knew that Watley wasn't the kind to back off once he started asking, Dylan gave him an abbreviated version of what had happened. "A woman went into labor."

Watley stopped fooling with the camera. "And you took her to the hospital?" he asked.

Dylan scanned the street below. Nothing out of the ordinary was happening at the Den of Thieves. This was the restaurant's busiest hour, but there was no one entering or leaving who aroused his suspicions. So far, none of the usual players in what was reported to be a money-laundering scheme were evident.

"It was too late for that." He took off the lid from his cup and dropped it on the table.

"So you did what?" Picking up the discarded lid, Watley dropped it into the empty box he'd converted into a wastebasket. "Helped her deliver?" he prompted.

"Yeah."

With his wife a brief six weeks away from delivery, Watley was facing his first time up as a new father. Thoughts of the restaurant they were staking out were forgotten. "So, what did it feel like? Holding that newborn in your hands? You did hold it, right?"

"Yes, I held her."

"Well, what was it like?"

"Messy."

Usually a very easygoing man, Watley threw his hands up in exasperation. "Dammit, McMorrow, you've got a heart made out of stone, you know that? There you were, with the miracle of life happening right in front of you and you're thinking of cleanup detail."

"Somebody has to." Dylan paused, taking a long sip of the coffee that was already getting cold. His thoughts kept returning to the event. He'd felt like a bystander and a participant all at the same time. "It was kind of strange," he finally added.

Watley's interest was instantly piqued. "Strange?"

"Like it wasn't real." Dylan looked at his partner. "Except that it was."

"Right." Watley slanted him a glance, then grinned. "That's probably the most eloquent I remember ever hearing you get."

Dylan didn't feel like being eloquent. He didn't feel like being anything but the cop he was being paid to be. It was too complicated any other way. Dylan nodded toward the building across the street. "Anything going on in there?"

Clearly bored, Watley shook his head. He took

the lid off the puzzle he'd brought with relish. "Nothing more than usual. I'm beginning to think this is just a wild-goose chase. Haven't seen any of the big boys go in or out yet. Maybe the tip was bogus. God only knows where that accountant disappeared to." The operation had begun in earnest on the word of one Owen Michelson, the restaurant's accountant. But neither he nor the information he'd promised had turned up at a rendezvous he'd arranged last week.

"Chambers said he thought he saw someone he recalled seeing on a poster going in this morning, but he's not sure," Watley remarked. Dumping out the puzzle's pieces on the table, Watley smiled to himself. "I think it's just wishful thinking on his part, but we sent a copy of the photo he took to the feds for positive ID."

"And?"

Watley shook his head. "Nothing yet."

Dylan blew out a breath. "And the wheels of justice turn slowly." He took another swig from his coffee before setting the cup down in disgust. It hardly met his criteria for coffee beyond being liquid. Restless, he ran his hand along the back of his neck and told himself to calm down. "Doesn't matter, we're not going anywhere." Watley groaned his agreement.

Dylan wished he had a cigarette.

Dylan pulled up the hand brake on his beat-up sports car. He'd bought it with the first money he'd earned the day before he left home. It still ran well. A single turn of his key cut off the engine and the low murmur of music that had been playing on the radio.

He sat in the stilled vehicle, looking at the back entrance to Harris Memorial and wondering if he'd lost his mind.

Getting off work half an hour ago, he'd had every intention of picking up some takeout at the new Thai restaurant near the stakeout and heading straight back to the place where he slept and ate when he wasn't on the job. It wasn't really home, but it served in lieu of one. Dylan hadn't thought of a place as being home since his mother had died.

But instead of doing that, somehow, he'd ended up here instead, with no takeout sitting on the seat beside him and no claim to sanity even remotely in the vicinity. The smart thing, he knew, was to send either Alexander or Hathaway here. They were the ones handling the case, not him.

He frowned, absently watching a couple rush through the electronic doors.

Lucy didn't need to see him again, it'd only upset her. And he sure as hell didn't need to see her again.

Dylan began to turn the key in the ignition, then stopped, silently cursing himself. He couldn't do it. There was a sense of right and wrong instilled in him, the one thing his mother managed to accomplish with her rebellious son.

He dragged his hand through his hair. It was his mother's fault that he was here.

And his father's fault that he shouldn't be.

C'mon, fish or cut bait, McMorrow.

Biting off another curse, Dylan got out of his car

and slammed the door shut behind him. Might as well get this over with, he thought.

As he strode almost militantly toward the bank of elevators located in the rear of the building, the hospital's small gift shop still managed to catch his eye. The little teddy bear with a jaunty pink bow over one ear in the center of the window display all but popped out at him. Stopping in midstride, he went in before he changed his mind.

The shop, with its cheerful clutter, was empty except for one other customer who was browsing on the opposite side.

"How much for the bear in the window?" Dylan asked.

His question, snapped out the way it was, startled the mature-looking, pink-smocked woman behind the counter. As she looked up, her features softened into a grandmotherly smile. "Twelve ninety-five."

Dylan dug into his front pocket. The wad of bills that comprised change from the twenty he'd given the cashier at the coffee shop earlier tumbled out onto the counter. He isolated the proper amount.

"I'll take it."

"And anything for the mother?"

Head snapping up, he looked at the woman sharply. "What makes you think…?"

The beatific smile was understanding. "You have that harried, new-father look about you."

The hell he did. The woman was probably just trying to push merchandise. Almost against his will, he saw the light blue negligee that hung just behind the woman on another display against the back wall. For a fleeting, insane moment, he was tempted. But then good sense returned.

"Just the bear."

"Fine." The woman accepted the money he handed her. "I'll ring it up for you. Would you like it wrapped?"

"The baby's only a few hours old, she wouldn't be able to unwrap anything," he answered stoically.

"Perhaps her mother—"

"No."

The woman inclined her head good-naturedly. "Very well, sir."

Three minutes later, Dylan was jabbing the up button at the elevator bank. When two elevators arrived at the same time, he chose the empty one, then pressed five. The steel doors closed, locking him in.

He had no idea what he'd say to Lucy.

Part of him hoped that she was asleep, that he could just place the teddy bear on some available surface in her room and retreat, saying he'd done his duty.

Getting off the elevator when it stopped on Lucy's floor, he made his way to her room. He should let someone else explain the cold details to her, he thought. It'd been a mistake to think he could handle it better than Alexander or Hathaway. A mistake to think that he could handle seeing her again. He made a left at the nurse's station. Coming back into her life, even for a few minutes, had been nothing short of disastrous.

That was why he'd left to begin with, to spare them both this kind of thing. No, he amended, grappling with an annoyance he couldn't quite trace to its roots, it'd been to spare her, not himself.

Nothing was going to spare him.

Arriving at her room, he eased the door open and peered in. Just as he'd hoped, she was asleep. Very softly, he entered the room, then slowly closed the door behind him.

For a second, Dylan stood there, just looking at Lucy. At the woman he'd once, fleetingly, thought of as his salvation. But he'd only been deluding himself. She deserved better than the future he could give her.

The late-afternoon sun illuminated the room, bathing everything it touched in shades of gold and whispering along her face and arms. The way his hand once had. She looked like the princess in that story his mother had told him years ago, when he'd been young and the world still held promise. The one where the princess slept in the glass casket, waiting to be woken up by her true love's first kiss.

It wouldn't be him she'd be waiting for, he thought.

As quietly as possible, he tiptoed over to the bed and placed the teddy bear on the table that was pushed over just to the side. Because he was in a hurry, his hand wasn't quite steady. As he took a step back, the bear toppled silently from the table, falling to the floor.

It figured. Dylan bent down quickly to retrieve it before Lucy woke up.

"Why don't you just hand it to me?"

Her voice, soft, filled with the last remnants of sleep, surrounded him. Their eyes met as he rose again. Unaccountably, he felt like a kid caught with his hand in a cookie jar.

"I didn't want to wake you."

"I wasn't asleep." With a hand digging into the

mattress on either side of her, Lucy pushed herself further up on the bed. "Just resting. The nurse just took Elena back."

"Elena?" His own voice sounded hopelessly dumb to his ear.

He looked edgy, she thought, like he didn't want to be here. Nothing had changed. "The baby."

"Elena." Dylan repeated the name slowly. Elaine had been his mother's name. He thought it an odd coincidence. "Nice name."

"I always thought so." She struggled to get past the awkward feeling. And the anger that was cutting off her words, her train of thought. She hadn't thought seeing him again would hurt so much. "It seems to suit her."

Dylan lifted a shoulder, letting it drop carelessly. He wouldn't know about that. Babies all tended to look alike to him, except that this one had a mop of dark hair.

Realizing he was still holding the teddy bear, he felt like a stuttering fool. He thrust it toward her, wanting to be out of here. "Well, I just came by to give you this for the baby—for Elena."

She took it from him, surprised that he could pick out something so sweet. But then, maybe it wasn't such a surprise. There had been sweet moments with him. Moments that had been left unguarded when he… She banked down the memory, the feelings. Reliving them would only stir things up more and she had spent all these months clearing them out of her life. "That's very nice of you."

"Yeah, well…" He began to edge out of the room.

"You didn't wait." Her eyes held his. "You promised you would."

Feeling uncomfortable in his own skin, he looked away. "I was late for work."

Lucy nodded. There would always be excuses between them. Excuses and lies. But now there would always be something more.

Setting the teddy bear aside on the table, she took a deep breath and pressed the button on the railing that raised her up into a sitting position. "Could you help me up, please?"

He stopped his retreat and looked at her in surprise. She was trying to get out of bed. What was wrong with her? "Look, I can get the nurse if you—"

Because she continued moving to the edge of the bed in small increments, he pushed the table out of the way and moved beside her, placing his hand to her back to keep her steady.

Only the fact that there was pain shooting through other parts of her kept Lucy from reacting to the feel of his hand along her back. "Sheila said I was supposed get out of bed later today and walk down the hall at least once."

He stared at her. "But you just gave birth. Well, not 'just,' but—" He was stumbling over his own tongue and it annoyed the hell out of him. "Isn't that a little barbaric?"

The journey to the edge of the bed, to where her legs were dangling over the side, seemed almost endless, but she finally made it, feeling a little triumphant at the accomplishment.

"They say it helps you heal faster."

She looked at him and tried not to let the fact

that his face was just inches away from hers affect her. Instead, she concentrated on the coldness she'd seen in his eyes the day he'd broken it off between them. Broken it off just when she'd thought they were building something lasting.

"Besides," she continued, "there's not going to be anyone to help once I get home, I need to get stronger." Her best friend had offered, but there was the store they co-owned to see to. That would keep Alma more than busy.

Seeing she was determined, Dylan offered her his arm. Some things, he thought, didn't change. Too bad Ritchie had never had her stubborn streak and stuck it out with something he'd begun. "You've always been the strongest person I knew."

She began to smile at the comment. Her smile tightened as her feet finally reached the floor and she tried to stand. Pain ricocheted through her.

He saw her wincing and stopped immediately. "I don't think this is such a good idea."

She clenched her teeth together. "Yes, it is. Just let me hold on to your arm." Biting her lower lip, she straightened and finally gained her feet.

It was then that he noticed. "You're barefoot. Wait a second." As gently as he could, Dylan eased her back onto the bed, then bent down to look under the bed. Except for a couple of wads of what looked like elastic-trimmed light blue tissue paper, there was nothing there. "Where're your slippers?"

"I don't have any. I came here unexpectedly, remember?" She curled her toes as more pain sought her out. She forced herself to think past it. "The hospital issued me paper ones. I think they're under there somewhere."

Snagging the only things he found, Dylan frowned as he straightened them out. They were slippers, all right—of a sort. "Don't see how these are going to make much of a difference."

"It's all I have right now." Lucy reached for them, but to her surprise, Dylan started to put them on her feet himself.

"You're better off not bending and struggling just yet," he explained gruffly. She might be tough, but she wasn't always the most sensible woman.

Like the time she'd whispered to him that she loved him.

Carefully, he eased the elastic back on first one, then the other as he slipped them on her feet. Standing up, he offered her his arm again.

She took it, careful to tuck the ends of her gown together. Lucy held them down by pressing her elbow against her side before she straightened again.

"No robe?" He glanced around the room and had his answer even as he asked.

"No robe," she confirmed. She felt wobbly and tried not to show it. "I've got a suitcase packed, but it's at home. In all the excitement, I forgot about it."

He should have taken that into account when the ambulance came for her. It was an oversight on his part. "Can't you call someone to bring it to you?"

There was Alma, but she was busy with the shop. For just a moment, her eyes touched his face before a curtain fell over them. Thoughts of her best friend faded into the background, nudged aside by memories of other times. "Not right now."

"I'll get it for you." He bit the words off. He glanced toward the door. From where he stood, it was a long distance from the bed if measured in pain-encased inches. He still thought she should be resting. "Ready?"

"Ready." Her voice quavered just a little as very slowly, Lucy took her first step away from the bed and toward the door.

Chapter 4

He'd thought he could contain it. Contain the question and just move on from there. Pretend it didn't even exist. But it did exist and he hadn't counted on it ebbing and flowing within him like a living force of nature, rising up like a tidal wave and threatening to wash over him and sweep him away entirely.

There was nothing he could do to stop it.

"Who's the father, Lucy?" he asked.

Just crossing the threshold leading out of her room, Lucy faltered. Though she'd known she would have to face the question from him soon enough, she hadn't expected it to be put to her so bluntly, without a preamble.

She kept her face forward, concentrating on her goal—the farthest corner of the nurses' station's outer desk. "Just someone I knew."

Every word stung him, leaving behind a mark

even though he told himself it shouldn't. After what had happened between them, how could she have gone on to someone else so quickly? "That casual?"

One step after another, she chanted mentally, watching her feet. "There was nothing casual about it, but it's over."

"He's not in your life anymore." It wasn't exactly a question, but an assumption. One he was very willing to make, though he knew it was selfish of him.

She wished he'd stop asking questions. He hadn't the right. "Not where it counts."

"Does he know about the baby?"

She thought of lying, but there were enough lies to keep track of. "No."

He never could leave things alone, he thought. Even when they were the way he wanted them. "Don't you think you should tell him?"

She spared him one glance before looking away again. "No. There're enough complications in both our lives without bringing that in, too. He's better off not knowing about the baby."

He couldn't believe that Lucy would keep something like this a secret. It seemed out of character for her. "Don't you think you owe it to Elena to let her father know she exists?"

There was anger in her eyes when she looked at him, reminding him of the passion he'd once seen there. Passion that had belonged to him at the time.

If she could have, she would have pulled her arm away from his. But she felt too unsteady to manage the gesture. The words, though, she could manage. "So that he can knowingly reject her? I don't think so. Better for that to remain a question than a fact.'' It cost her dearly to pull her shoulders back, but she did. ''I don't want to talk about this anymore, all right?''

She had a right to her privacy. He'd always insisted on his. They'd been lovers for less than two-thirds of a year, but she'd never known anything about his family other than the few vague answers he'd given her. ''All right.''

She made the next few steps in silence, nodding at the nurse who walked by them and smiled. Lucy knew from experience that Dylan could keep his own council indefinitely. ''But I do want to talk.''

He heard the note in her voice and knew what it was about. ''I figured.''

''Tell me about Ritchie.'' Though it hurt to think of her brother being dead, she forced herself to ask. ''How did he die?''

She was still weak. Otherwise, he knew she wouldn't be hanging on to him so tightly. He didn't want to add to what she was already going through. ''Lucy, this isn't the time—''

She wasn't going to let him put her off any longer. And she had a right to know what had happened to her brother. ''It's never the time to hear that someone you loved is dead.'' Lucy turned her face toward Dylan. ''How did he die?''

''He was shot. At close range. They found him in an irrigation ditch near the farmland,'' he said.

The city stood on the site of what had once been a huge farming estate owned by the Bedford family for several generations. Now there were only small, sporadic patches left. Located in the western end of

Bedford, they were still coaxing forth crops of corn, strawberries and, in a few places, oranges.

Lucy looked at him, the halting progress she was making temporarily aborted. "Farmland? Ritchie would have never been there. He never liked anything remotely rural."

Dylan tended to agree with her. The Ritchie he knew was far more likely to be found in clubs and wherever there were bright lights.

"He was killed somewhere else, then dum—left in the ditch." Dylan caught himself at the last minute, steering clear of the detached language he usually used in referring to victims and suspects. It served to maintain his perspective. Attachments only got in the way of judgment.

But in this case, he couldn't let himself be clinically detached. To be that way was disrespectful to the friendship he and Ritchie had once had, however fleeting.

Besides, he didn't really need to be detached here, it wasn't his case to solve. Only to relate. So far, in his opinion, he was doing a damn poor job of it.

"According to the medical examiner, Ritchie died sometime around seven-thirty this morning. Do you know where he was supposed to be at seven-thirty?"

Lucy's expression froze. She knew exactly where he was at seven-thirty this morning. She knew because he was doing it for her. "He was going in to work early so that he could get the time off to take me to the doctor."

Dylan knew what she was thinking. Separation

hadn't dulled his ability to read her thoughts. "It's not your fault."

"Isn't it?" Her eyes filled with tears, which she kept from spilling out through sheer force of will. She didn't deserve the comfort of tears. Ritchie had died because of her. "If he hadn't gone in early for me, maybe he'd still be alive."

"And maybe he would have just been killed later." He wanted to shield her, but at the same time, he wanted to strip away her guilt. He told her the rest of it. "Lucy, Ritchie was shot execution-style." One bullet to the back of the head. It seemed surreal when he thought about it. Who could Ritchie have run afoul of for that to happen? He saw the horror in Lucy's face and pressed on. "That means it was done on purpose. He didn't just wander in on a burglary gone awry, or a car-jacking that went sour. Somebody meant to kill him." Impatience clawed at him. There were too many people around. "Can we go back to your room? This isn't the kind of thing to talk about strolling through the hospital halls."

"I wouldn't exactly considered this strolling," Lucy answered evenly.

She was trying very hard not to let her emotions break through. Inside, it felt as if she had a pressure cooker on, full of steam, ready to explode. Digging her fingers into his arm, she turned around to face the long trip back to her room.

The pace was getting to him. He'd never been one to hurry things along normally, but there was nothing normal about this. "Why don't I just carry you back? It'd save time."

Lucy blocked his hand as he moved to pick her up. "No," she snapped. "I can do this."

She didn't want him holding her. Not if she could avoid it. If he held her now, she would lose her strength and just dissolve against him, sobbing her heart out. She'd encountered enough setbacks in her life today as it was. She wasn't about to set herself up for more.

Annoyance at her stubbornness warred with a grudging admiration for her grit. Dylan managed to curb his impatience until they'd returned to the door of her room. But once he opened it, he swept her up into his arms and carried her the rest of the way.

"What are you doing?" She was almost too exhausted to offer a protest.

"Cutting about forty minutes off the trip back to your bed." Dylan caught himself thinking she still felt as if she weighed next to nothing.

He had her back in her bed in little more than four quick strides.

"Everything all right in here?"

Turning around, Dylan saw a nurse with salt-and-pepper hair in the doorway, peering into the room. She looked from him to Lucy.

"Fine," Lucy assured her. "I just got a little tired. It was my first time out of bed."

The nurse nodded knowingly. "Shouldn't try to do too much first time up." And then she smiled, her eyes washing over Dylan before they came to rest on Lucy. "A lady could do worse than have a handsome man carry her around."

With a wink aimed at Lucy, she left, closing the door behind her.

Dylan moved back from her bed as she slowly

toed off the slippers from her feet one at a time. The effort almost drained the remainder of her energy. She moved her legs under the covers, relieved to be lying down again.

With a sigh, she looked up at him. "Do you think you'll catch whoever killed Ritchie?"

He didn't answer her directly. "It's not my case."

She didn't understand. "Then why…?"

He was asking himself the same thing. "I thought it might be easier on you, hearing the news from me." Dylan shrugged carelessly. "Obviously I miscalculated. I hadn't figured on you being pregnant."

The coldness in his voice sliced through her. Defenses locked into place. "We can't always factor in everything. So, who *is* handling Ritchie's case? Do they have any leads?"

"Detectives Alexander and Hathaway, and they're not even sure where he was killed, yet. There was no blood at the crime scene, so he was moved." He went with the obvious first. "You said Ritchie was working. Where?"

"At a restaurant. He's a—was a waiter." Her mouth curved slightly. "He said they call them servers now."

Yeah, they did. Another attempt at depersonalizing everything, Dylan thought. He would have said it was a good thing, but there were times he wasn't sure. Being anesthetized was close to being dead, and he'd felt dead for a long time.

Except for the time he'd spent with Lucy.

But all that was over now. He'd made his peace

with the fact. He just had to remember that, that's all.

"Do you know where Ritchie worked?"

She nodded. "It's called Den of Thieves." He was staring at her. His face was impassive, but she could see that she had caught him by surprise. She wanted to know why. "What?"

It was a hell of a coincidence. "Are you sure that's where he worked?"

Why did he doubt her? "Yes, I'm sure. A friend of his got the job for him."

"Who?"

"I don't know, Ritchie didn't give me a name. Just someone he knew." She should have pressed harder for an answer. She should have done so many things differently. Her eyes met Dylan's. "Someone he said owed him a favor and this was his way of paying him back." And then she remembered something. "I don't know if this means anything or not—"

His eyes pinned her down, the detective in him coming out despite efforts to the contrary. "Let me be the one to decide."

She tried to get the words just right. "A couple of days ago, Ritchie told me he was on to something. Something that would put us in the money and on the right side of things for a long time to come." Taking a dim view of his schemes, she'd told him to forget about it then. But Ritchie had been too stubborn to listen.

"Did he say what?" Dylan asked.

She shook her head. "You know Ritchie, he gets—got—excited over things." It was so hard to think of him in the past tense. She wasn't sure just how she could bear it. "But he always played them close to his chest if they weren't completely above-board. He said there was no reason for me to know, too. That's what made me think it was dangerous." She bit her lip, taking a deep breath. It didn't ease the ache in her chest, or the one in her throat. "I told him that I didn't want him doing anything illegal and he said he wasn't the one standing on the wrong side of the law." Despite her best efforts, a tear spilled out, followed by another. She brushed them away with the back of her hand. "That's what got him killed, wasn't it?"

He curbed the desire to wipe away her tears. The word *no* hovered on his lips, but he tried to avoid lies whenever possible. The only lie he'd ever told Lucy was that he didn't love her.

"Possibly."

He was going to have to get back to Alexander and Hathaway on this. As well as Watley. Den of Thieves was suddenly one man short. The task force could use this information to their advantage. Could plant one of their own men inside.

The fact that he was using this tragedy as a tool to further the investigation disgusted him, but he knew that ignoring it couldn't help Ritchie now. And there was far more at stake here than just a dead man's sister's feelings and his own personal code of ethics. Other people's lives were involved. Innocent people.

"What exactly did Ritchie say to you?" He saw that she didn't understand where he was going with this. "Did he physically have something, some kind of evidence that he was going to blackmail someone with?"

Things began to crystallize in Dylan's mind. A few weeks ago, the accountant for Den of Thieves, Michelson, had approached the local D.A., saying that the restaurant was a front for money laundering. But the man had vanished without a trace before any sort of case could be made. If for some reason the person Ritchie was looking to blackmail was Alfred Palmero, the owner of the restaurant, it would go a long way toward explaining things.

Lucy shook her head, frustrated. "I don't know. He wasn't specific."

Dylan wondered how much he could tell Lucy about this, then decided that for her own protection, and that of the child she'd just given birth to, she needed to know at least some of it.

Because he knew he had a tendency to be far too blunt, Dylan tried to pick his words more carefully this time. "If he was looking to blackmail his boss, Alfred Palmero, your brother made the mistake of getting in over his head."

"Your brother," she echoed, looking at Dylan with disbelief. Could he really be that cold? Of course he could. Why did the fact keep surprising her? "You make it sound as if you didn't know him."

Damned if he did, damned if he didn't. "Lucy, I was just —"

But she was tired and angry and more than a little fed up. With him, with everything. All the hurt she felt finally made her temper snap.

"Keeping your distance, yes, I know. The way you do with everything. With me, with him, with life. You're very good at that. Keeping your distance. Protecting yourself at all costs." She was through crying over him. "Look, I don't need you coming into my life right now, disrupting everything. Thank you very much for coming by, for helping me, but I'd really just rather not see you again, all right?"

Dylan felt his own temper fraying. But he knew she had a right to what she was saying. "Sure, fine. I understand."

The thing of it was, he thought as he walked out, that he did understand. He would have probably played it the same way she had and for the same reason. For self-preservation.

But he still couldn't shake the image of Lucy's expression from his mind.

He supposed that it was exactly that image, playing itself over and over again in his mind's eye, that made him drive past his own apartment complex and keep right on going until he found himself turning down her street.

Though he tried to shake himself free of it, he felt as if he needed to make some sort of atonement. The least he could do was bring Lucy her suitcase. A woman needed things at a time like this. Things to make her feel less depersonalized, more human. Like her own nightgown and her own slippers.

Dylan couldn't give her anything else she needed, but at least he could give her a little of her outer dignity back. The hospital gowns certainly did little to preserve it.

Admittedly flimsy, it was the excuse he fed himself. It was the best he could do on short notice.

Holding on to it, Dylan parked his car in her driveway. The automatic sensors he'd insisted on putting up for her when they were still together turned on, illuminating his path. Feeling in his pocket for what he thought of as his skeleton keys, he noted a fresh oil slick on the asphalt beside his vehicle. He'd parked in the street earlier. The slick hadn't been there then. Dylan wondered if the ambulance had an oil leak and if someone had alerted the paramedics to it.

The front door wasn't locked.

The door gave the moment he inserted the thin metal wand into the keyhole and gave it the slightest bit of pressure.

He distinctly remembered shutting the door behind him this morning and hearing the tumbler click into place. As a cop, he'd been careful not to leave the house susceptible to invasion.

Something wasn't right.

Very slowly, Dylan turned the knob and then released it, clearing the doorsill. He moved the door away by inches, simultaneously feeling for his service revolver. Drawing it out, he took off the safety as quietly as possible and entered the house.

The living room looked as if a tornado had been through it.

Moving from room to room at an even pace, his gun poised, ready, Dylan took it all in. If at first glance he'd entertained the thought that this had been a run-of-the-mill break-in, the fact that the television set and audio equipment had been left behind quickly squelched the supposition. Lucy's house had been systematically tossed.

From all appearances, someone had wanted something very much. Since every room had been ransacked, Dylan's guess was that they hadn't found what they were looking for.

Satisfied that whoever had done this was long gone by now, he holstered his gun. All he could think of was that he was grateful Lucy and her baby hadn't been here at the time.

"What the hell were they looking for, Lucy?" he murmured to himself. "And what was it that Ritchie had on them?"

He realized that he'd made a leap in judgment, but his gut told him that there was a connection here between where Ritchie worked and what had happened to the house. His gut instincts were rarely wrong.

The question still remained. What?

Lucy was going to have a fit when she saw this, he thought, pressing the numbers on his cell phone that would connect him to the precinct. Maybe forensics would come up with a few answers for them.

Hanging up a few minutes later, he looked around for the suitcase he'd come for originally. He found it in Lucy's bedroom, its jaws yawning wide open, its contents scattered in a rude semicircle around it. He'd have to wait for forensics to go over the crime scene before he could remove the suitcase and the few things he judged had been in it. With a sigh, he made himself as comfortable as possible.

"Your timing is perfect, she just finished her dinner," Lucy said, looking up from the sleeping infant at her breast. Expecting to see the nurse, her smile faded when she saw Dylan entering her room.

Primly, she covered herself, her mouth hardening. Why couldn't he leave her alone and let her heal?

"I didn't expect to see you again."

Her voice was cool, distant. He couldn't blame her. Dylan nodded at the suitcase he was holding, telling himself that the sight of Lucy nursing her baby didn't effect him one way or another.

"I thought you might need some things." He placed it at the end of her bed.

"What are you trying to do to me, Dylan? Why are you being nice to me one minute, then the next...?"

Abruptly, Lucy caught hold of herself, breaking off her words midsentence. There was no point in upbraiding him, and she refused to lose her composure in front of her daughter, no matter how young the girl was. She had to be strong and this wasn't the way.

With effort, Lucy regrouped, then looked at the suitcase as he flipped open the locks. Maybe, in his own way, he was trying. At least she could be civil toward him. "Thank you."

He picked up the lid for her, opening the case. "I wasn't sure if you needed anything else."

Her eyes narrowed as she looked into the contents. Instead of the orderly packing she'd done, everything was jumbled up inside, as if it had been through a spin cycle in a dryer. Why had he gone through her things? "What did you do to it?"

"Nothing." It wasn't going to be any easier to tell her this part than it had about Ritchie, but he struggled to find a way. "I just threw in what I thought you could use."

She raised her eyes to his, confused. "I don't

understand. I packed my suitcase two weeks ago.'' A day before her due date, she remembered. ''How did it get like this?''

''Someone unpacked it.''

''You?'' The accusation was impossible to miss.

''No.'' He blew out a breath, wishing that for once in his life, he had another way with words than just spitting them out like an automatic weapon. But nothing came to him except the naked truth.

''Lucy, somebody broke into your house and ransacked it.''

Chapter 5

His words made her feel vulnerable and naked. Completely defenseless and at the mercy of a whimsical fate that was not known for its kindness.

For a long moment, only the soft sound of Elena's even breathing as she slept disturbed the silence that hung heavily in the room.

Lucy shook her head in disbelief. "You know, I'm really beginning to dread seeing you walk in. First you tell me that Ritchie's dead, now you tell me my house was burglarized—"

"No," he said, quick to correct her, "not burglarized, broken into. As far as I could tell, they didn't take anything."

Maybe she still wasn't connecting all the dots after what she'd been through, but that didn't make any sense to her. "But then why...?"

"It looks as if they were looking for something."

"What?"

"I don't know. At first glance, it doesn't look as if anything was taken, but only you could be the judge of that." Although, he did have his suspicions as to what was the object of the search. Even though everything within her house had been thrown into complete chaos, he'd noticed that particular attention seemed to have been paid to her videotape collection. Each one of them had been ripped from its cover.

Her confusion came to a skidding halt as her thoughts converged on the only plausible explanation she could come up with.

Lucy bit her lower lip. Almost reflexively, her arms tightened around her sleeping baby. "Ritchie?"

"Probably." Pulling the lone chair in the room closer to her bed, he sat down next to her. "Whatever he had on someone, it looks like he might have had physical proof." Hesitating, Dylan made a judgment call. It wasn't the way the captain would have wanted him to play it, but the captain didn't know Lucy the way he did. It was time to tell her a few things. "Ritchie was working for a place that's being investigated."

This was all beginning to sound hopelessly farfetched. Things like this didn't happen in real life, only the mysteries she used to love to lose herself in. "Investigated by whom? The police?"

He nodded. That's the way it had begun. Now it was a joint venture. "And the Justice Department."

"But why? Drugs? Illegal firearms?" None of it made sense to her.

"You're better off not knowing that" was all he said to her. She knew by the set of his mouth that she'd get no more out of him. Lucy was surprised he's said as much as he had.

"You're serious about this, aren't you? About there being something dangerous going on." Even as she voiced her skepticism, she saw her answer in Dylan's expression.

"Very."

She'd been to the restaurant on several occasions in the short time Ritchie worked there. To pick him up from work when his car was in the shop and once to celebrate his birthday. It had seemed like a nice place and she'd been impressed by it. It was built to look like something out of the Arabian Nights, the interior was bright and trendy. On Ritchie's birthday, the owner, Alfred Palmero, had come out to personally wish him a happy birthday and slip him a little something in an envelope. It had been a check for a hundred dollars. It had seemed a little out of place to her at the time, but people took to Ritchie and she thought it wasn't anything more than that. Palmero had seemed genuinely fond of her brother. On that night, he'd told her that he had plans for Ritchie's advancement.

Ritchie had looked a little uncomfortable at the time, but she'd thought that was because he never liked being confronted with anything permanent. Ritchie liked moving from job to job as well as from woman to woman. Nothing held his interest for very long. That was what had made him Ritchie.

She couldn't believe what Dylan was telling her. "And you think that the people there are somehow involved in Ritchie's death?"

Dylan had no proof of any kind, just a vague statement, acquired secondhand, a few too many coincidences by his count and a gut feeling he wasn't about to ignore. It wouldn't have made a case in front of the feeblest of juries.

He went a little farther out on a limb. "A few weeks ago, the restaurant's accountant asked for a private meeting with the D.A. The allegations he made were pretty much what was already suspected. But he added that he had the proof to back him up."

What did all this have to do with Ritchie? she wondered. "What happened?"

He gave her the shortened version. He didn't want her completely in the dark, but the less details she knew, the better off she was. "The meeting that was set up never came off. The accountant disappeared without a trace. He wasn't the kind of man to just pull a vanishing act. He left behind a sizable bank account, not to mention a family. They haven't heard from him since he failed to show up at the meeting."

Lucy shivered in the warm room. "And you think he's dead?"

Dylan didn't want to frighten her, but he wouldn't insult her with a lie, either. "I'd say it was a pretty safe bet."

She tried to take in what he was saying to her. "And you think Ritchie might have somehow been involved in all this? Ritchie would have never—"

He spared her having to say it. They both knew Ritchie would have never had anything to do with murder. "I know."

But Ritchie *had* been somehow involved. Looking back, she supposed that would explain a lot.

Ritchie's evasiveness, his being so sure that things were going to turn around for them soon. *Oh, damn, Ritchie, how could you have gotten yourself mixed up in this? Why didn't you just walk away?*

Dylan saw the pain in her eyes and wished there was something he could do or say to erase it instead of increasing it. But then, he'd never been very good for her. He'd always known that. "At this point, I'd say there was a definite possibility that he was somehow involved in all this. I just don't know how." He paused, thinking. He didn't like the idea of her being alone. "Do you have anyone you can stay with?"

There was Alma, but there was hardly enough room for Alma and her things within her tiny studio apartment, much less for another woman with a baby.

She shook her head. And then the impact of his question hit. Her eyes widened. "You think they'll be back?"

There was no way to sugarcoat this. For her safety, he didn't even try. "If they didn't find what they were after, yes."

She looked down at the sleeping infant in her arms. "I'll get a large dog." She'd been meaning to get one for protection for a while now. This just made it necessary.

Dylan frowned. She was going to need more than just a dog. A dog could easily be disposed of. "I'll see what I can do about getting you some police protection."

She wanted more than protection, she wanted revenge. Lucy raised her eyes to his. "If you think that Palmero is somehow responsible for Ritchie's death, can't you do something about it?''

The breath he blew out was one of frustration. ''We need evidence, and evidence takes time.''

Much as he wanted to reassure her that something would be done, he wasn't at liberty to explain just what they were doing or his part in it. This was an on-going investigation, and Lucy's knowing any more about it would endanger all of them, not just him.

Dylan glanced at his watch. It was getting late. He had to be going. She needed her rest and he needed not to be standing here, looking at her. Old memories had a way of permeating no matter what sort of a defensive he was mounting against them.

He indicated her suitcase. ''In the meantime. I thought you might want some of your own things.'' He noticed the way the hospital gown slid off her shoulder. He remembered how soft her skin had felt beneath his hand. ''Not that the hospital gown isn't without merit.''

Lucy pushed the gown back up, feeling herself growing warm. He'd always had that effect on her, creating intimacy in the middle of chaos.

And distance in the middle of intimacy, she reminded herself.

She looked at the jumble in the suitcase. There was no reason for Dylan to have gone out of his way like this for her. Especially after the way she'd thrown him out of her room earlier.

''That was very nice of you.'' She raised her eyes to his, wishing with all her heart that things were different. But they weren't, she silently reminded herself. "Dylan, I didn't mean to snap at you when you came in."

"Who better than you?" There was a bare hint of a smile as he shrugged philosophically. "Way I see it, you've earned the right." He rose to his feet, then paused, held fast by things that weren't visible. Things that could only be felt. "I'm very sorry about Ritchie. He was a good guy."

"Yes," she agreed softly. "He was." She stroked Elena's jet-black hair, struggling with the lump in her throat. "You know, he was really looking forward to this baby. Maybe even more than I was. Kept telling me not to worry, that it was going to be all right." A bittersweet smile played on her lips. "He liked to talk about all the things he was going to do with the baby once it was born." Tears welled up in her eyes, spilling out. "And now she'll never get to know him." Lucy pressed her lips together, unable to continue.

The tears undid him. He remembered other tears, and the same helpless feeling eating away at him. Dylan forgot about the distance he was trying to maintain.

His hand beneath her chin, he raised her head until her eyes met his. "Hey, now, don't do that. It won't help anything," Dylan told her softly.

Embarrassed at the loss of control, Lucy wiped her damp cheeks with the back of her hand.

"You're right, Ritchie wouldn't have wanted to be remembered this way. He would have wanted me to toast his newest venture." Lucy raised her eyes toward the ceiling. "Though I don't think heaven's going to really be ready for him."

"You're probably right." The Ritchie he remembered had been too full of life and too full of energy to be fitted for a set of angel's wings. "But since we're talking about Ritchie…" Dylan began quietly. "Unless something unexpected turns up in the autopsy, his body's going to be released early tomorrow morning." With Lucy still in the hospital, that complicated things. "I could see about making his funeral arrangements for you."

Her immediate reaction was to say no, that she could take care of her own, thank you. But both of them knew that for the moment, she obviously couldn't. To refuse him because of her stubborn pride would be stupid. And, after all, he had been Ritchie's friend. If she set aside her own differences with Dylan, she could see that her brother's death had affected him.

In hindsight, Dylan had probably been the best friend Ritchie had ever had. It was their breakup, hers and Dylan's, that had caused Ritchie to back away from him.

Maybe if he hadn't, he would have still been alive now.

Lucy sighed. There was no sense in torturing herself this way. It wouldn't change anything. If nothing else, what had happened between her and Dylan had taught her that.

"Thank you, I would appreciate that," she told him quietly.

He doubted if she actually meant the words she used, but he knew Lucy was far too practical in her own way to refuse an offer that made sense, no matter what her feelings about him might be. It was his guess that they were probably as strong now as they had once been, only now they were of a different venue.

She'd loved him once and he had turned his back on her. It had been for her own good, even if he'd never told her that. She wouldn't have understood if he had, would have probably tried to talk him out of it if she'd known everything.

Now those strong feelings were probably given over to another emotion, equally as passionate. He only had to think of his father to know that love and hate could coexist. And only think of his mother to know that one could destroy the other.

It was best not to go there. There was nothing to be gained from it.

He heard the nurse entering the room behind him. He'd overstayed his visit.

"All right, then, I'll take care of it," he promised. In light of everything, it was the least he could do.

"More personal time?" Watley said, looking up from the book he was only half reading. He set his book down on the edge of the card table and looked at Dylan. "Wow, twice in three days. You keep this up and people are going to start saying you actually have a life."

Lucy was being discharged this afternoon, despite her doctor siding with Dylan and advising her to remain an extra day. She needed someone to bring her home. He'd decided that that someone was him. Dylan had done it all by the book, informing his captain and now Watley that he was taking several hours of personal time.

He didn't need to be razzed. "I never cared much

about what people have to say, one way or another.''

''It's the sister, isn't it?'' Watley asked.

The look Dylan slanted his way would have made a lesser man cower in uncertainty. He'd filled Watley in on what he'd told the captain and the others on the task force, as well as Alexander and Hathaway. That the homicide victim who had been discovered three days earlier was most likely connected to the Palmero investigation. Dylan had been brief in his summation, skipping the part that Ritchie Alvarez wouldn't have been above a little blackmail when it involved the bad guys. In Dylan's estimation they would have had to have known Ritchie in order to understand and not condemn.

He figured Ritchie had already paid the ultimate price. There was no need to drag his name through the mud.

Or Lucy's, either.

Dylan had also been brief describing his connection to the man and to his family, namely his sister, Lucy. He definitely had omitted that they'd once been involved. It had no bearing on anything. He should have figured that Watley, a terminally incurable romantic trapped in the body of a lumbering bear, would have picked up on that somehow.

''Yes, it's the sister,'' he said evenly. ''She needs police protection. I already told you that. I'm bringing her and her baby home from the hospital, nothing more.''

Watley appeared to be taking it all in, nodding thoughtfully. ''What about the father?''

It was a question Dylan kept coming back to

himself. He shrugged. "She says he's out of the picture."

Watley didn't look convinced. "Make sure he's not the jealous type."

The offhanded advice struck a chord deep within Dylan. It would have been cruelly ironic if Lucy had become involved with someone given to fits of jealousy. Heading toward the door, he glanced over his shoulder as he dismissed Watley's warning.

"Don't worry about that." Dylan stopped. There was an odd expression on Watley's face, as if his partner was choking back on a grin he was trying to swallow. "What's with you?"

"It's nothing." Watley pretended to try to compose himself. "It just always chokes me up, watching a fledgling leaving the nest for the first time."

Dylan's eyes narrowed. "If you don't watch your step, I'll burn the nest down around you."

Giving up the effort, Watley laughed out loud. "Does she know about that temper of yours?"

The hint of a smile faded. Dylan opened the door. "She knows all she needs to know."

"Somehow," Watley said under his breath as the apartment door closed, "I tend to doubt that. Good luck, lady. You're going to need it." Pushing his book aside, he got up to monitor the camera.

There was no denying that Dylan had gone far out of his way. He'd brought her her clothes, seen to Ritchie's funeral arrangements and provided not only a ride home, but even an infant seat for the baby. She wouldn't have believed him to be this thoughtful, even while she'd been in love with him.

But there was also no denying the fact that she

felt uneasy here sitting next to him in the car. Uneasy because all the available space in the small enclosure was filled with memories and feelings that had once been left out in the cold when he had walked away from her and the life she thought they could have together.

Uneasy because she knew how susceptible she was to another onslaught of those same feelings. And being engulfed by those feelings would make her nothing short of stupid, because this time wouldn't play any differently than the last.

It was a given. She knew that. Nothing about Dylan had changed.

She supposed that was part of the problem. Dylan *hadn't* changed. He was still the same man she'd fallen in love with.

But she had changed, she reminded herself. Pain had made her grow, made her abandon the Pollyanna outlook she had once embraced and brought her face-to-face with reality. It had changed her. And knowing she was to be a mother had changed her. It had made her stronger, more independent. More determined to stand on her own two feet no matter what. Because there wasn't just herself to think of anymore.

This time, she wasn't going to be a fool.

Silence had never bothered him before. Given his choice, he had always preferred silence to sound. His own council to the noise of others. But it was different this time. This time, the silence only underscored the lack of something.

The lack of the sound of her voice.

"You're usually more talkative than this." He caught the careless rise of her shoulder out of the corner of his eye. He couldn't explain why that bothered him as much as it did. He felt as if he'd lost something. "Thinking about Ritchie?"

Lucy kept her eyes straight ahead, venturing only to look in the rearview mirror to check on Elena. The baby was asleep, lulled by the movement of the vehicle.

"No, trying not to think about Ritchie. Trying to wrap my mind around the future."

Because it was by thinking of the future, by removing herself from the present, that she was going to be able to get through all this without crumbling. She couldn't allow herself to think about her brother's funeral. Or about sitting here beside Dylan and not reaching out to touch him. Not baring her soul to him the way she once had so naturally.

But all that, she reminded herself, had only been one-sided. She'd bared her soul to Dylan, but he had hardly allowed her a toehold into his own world, giving her only vague answers whenever she asked about his past or his family. All he'd told her was that his parents were dead. It had made her think that he needed her all the more.

Just went to show how naive someone in love could be, she thought.

"You'll get through it," he assured her. "If anyone can, you can."

"Yeah, that's me, the strong one." So why did she feel so damn vulnerable now?

He heard the sarcasm in her voice. It surprised him. He wouldn't have thought her capable of it. It made him wonder if the father of her child had done something to crush her spirit. He had to work at curbing the sudden flash of anger.

"Ritchie used to say he wished he was as strong as his little sister."

The casual reference coaxed a smile from her, fondness curving her mouth. "Ritchie just liked to talk." Lucy closed her eyes, remembering far better days. "He could have been anything he wanted to be, but he liked being what he was." She opened her eyes again and looked at Dylan. "Rootless."

"Oh, I don't know." She had no idea what rootless was, he thought. He was the rootless one, not Ritchie. "He felt pretty attached to you."

She began to protest, then stopped. There was really no denying that, she realized. She and Ritchie had had a bond, no matter how much they had argued. "And to his friends."

Like the one who had gotten him his job with Den of Thieves, Dylan thought grimly. His laugh was short, humorless. "Ritchie's problem was that he wasn't always careful about his choice of friends."

That much was true, but she felt compelled to defend her brother now that he could no longer do it himself. "He liked people. Liked to see the good in them."

Dylan heard her daring him to dispute that. He wasn't about to try. "He once told me that he picked that up from you."

She couldn't help the smile that came to her. "Funny, I thought I got it from him." The sadness she was trying so desperately to ignore threatened to overwhelm her again. "I'm going to miss him a lot."

Because they were stopped at a light and emotion was running high within the limited space of the car, Dylan allowed himself one unguarded moment. He slipped his hand over hers, squeezing it slightly. It was all he could allow himself to do.

''Yeah, me, too.''

The surprised look in her eyes when she turned her head toward him faded after a beat, replaced with a smile that seemed to filter slowly down to her lips.

There were times, she knew, when he could seem very kind. It helped to know that they shared at least this much. ''Thank you.''

And then she went with the moment. Lucy wasn't sure exactly what prompted her, but she leaned over the lowered hand brake and kissed his cheek.

Caught unprepared, a familiar sweetness poured all through Dylan. Everything within him gravitated toward it like victims of a shipwreck to the only raft bobbing in the water. Belatedly, he tried to block the feeling, but it was too late. So he let himself enjoy it.

Just this once.

The driver behind them leaned on his horn, tearing the moment apart.

Just as well, Dylan thought. Personal time or not, he still felt as if he was on duty. Being on duty didn't include indulging himself or giving in to a sudden onslaught of needs, no matter how unexpected or demanding.

He kept repeating that to himself as he drove the rest of the way to her house.

It helped.

But not much.

Chapter 6

Lucy stood to the side as Dylan put down her suitcase and the infant seat and unlocked the front door for her. Holding Elena tightly in her arms, she braced herself for the shambles that she was about to see, the harsh evidence of strange hands rifling through her things, through her life.

She tried very hard not to dwell on how violated, how vulnerable that made her feel. It seemed to her that everything was conspiring to make her feel that way, but she just wasn't going to allow it. Not for her sake, not for Elena's. She refused to be vulnerable.

Like someone about to dive into the deep end of the pool, she took a deep breath and entered. If he hadn't been paying attention, Dylan would have walked right into her when she stopped dead in the doorway.

Everything was just the way she'd left it.

Enormously confused, she turned around to look over her shoulder at Dylan. "I thought you said someone broke in."

Shutting the door behind him, he walked around Lucy and put down the suitcase just inside the room. He'd leave its final destination up to her. The infant seat he placed on the coffee table.

"They did."

He'd said the place had been ransacked. Didn't that mean that things had been tossed around, left in utter disarray? Burglars didn't neaten up after themselves. What was going on here?

"But it doesn't look like it," she insisted. It wasn't like Dylan to try to scare her. Why had he said what he'd said?

He shrugged, feeling awkward. Why couldn't she be more like a man and just let things ride? Accept things in stride. Why did she force him to admit things? "I kind of fixed things up."

Elena started to fuss. Lucy began rocking her slightly as she continued to stare at him. "You?" She couldn't picture him picking up anything.

"After the forensics team left." He was beginning to regret having done anything. He shoved his hands into his back pockets. "I figured you had enough on your mind without coming home to a place that looked as if it had been struck by a tornado."

A sweetness filtered in, wedging aside the iron bars of her resolve the way nothing else could have. He'd gone out of his way, done something that was entirely alien to his frame of reference. For her.

She just stood there, staring at him. Waiting for it to make sense. "So you cleaned up."

"Something like that."

Lucy sighed, shaking her head. It was beginning to ache. "You know, you never really cease to amaze me. I just can't figure you out."

His eyes met hers. He refused to read what was within them. That way lay only trouble. "Maybe you shouldn't try."

The laugh was short, but not completely devoid of humor. "What, and give up a lifelong challenge?" Lucy faced him squarely, making a promise only half in jest. "Someday, Dylan, I do intend to have your number."

The way he figured it, she already did, she just didn't know it. And he meant to keep it that way. For both their sakes. It was the only way.

He'd forgotten how hard it was to really block her from his mind, how to keep little things from seeping in. Like the way one side of her mouth rose just a little higher than the other when she smiled at him. Half-cocky, half-shy—and all Lucy.

He remembered that now, remembered how there were so many ways she could get to him. As many ways as there were moments in a day. The recollection didn't make him happy. It made life too difficult for him.

And life was about to get even more difficult after he told her what he had to say, but there was no putting it off.

"I'm going to be staying here tonight." And probably several more nights to come, he added silently, but he figured that was a little too much to lay on her now. And maybe too much to hear himself say as well. He needed to adjust, to get accustomed to the idea of being around her and not having it affect him.

Good luck, fella, he thought sarcastically.

Lucy was positive she couldn't have heard him right. "What?"

She looked, he thought, as if he'd just told her she had to spend the night with three of the FBI's top-ten most-wanted criminals. It bothered him even though he knew he should have been relieved. As long as she harbored ill feelings, there was no chance of anything renewing between them.

"The department's shorthanded and we can't spare too many people. The guy out front guarding the house right now is an off-duty detective who owes me a favor. We've got a lot of personnel tied up with other things, so I figured that I'd put my time in when I go off duty."

It was almost as if the baby could feel her agitation filtering through to her. Elena's fussing was taking on insistent proportions. Lucy began stroking the downy black hair on the infant's head. But her eyes were on Dylan.

"This isn't necessary."

"Yes," he told her firmly, "it is." This wasn't negotiable. "Someone broke in here looking for something. I've got a hunch they didn't find it. If they didn't, they might be back."

It was a chilling thought. But even more chilling was the idea of spending the night under the same roof with Dylan. She'd always thought of herself as a strong woman, but strength could only be stretched so far, tested so much, before it snapped and failed. Lucy raised her chin. "I can take care of myself."

His eyes lowered to look at Elena. His implication was clear. "And the baby?"

He was right and she should be grateful for his concern instead of fighting him. They'd had a past, but that's just what it was, the past. In the past. She had to get over any residual feelings and move on.

It wasn't going to be easy.

Lucy bit back a sigh. So who said life was supposed to be easy?

"All right." Her voice was stiff, almost formal. "Thank you."

She sounded like a stranger, he thought. It was probably better that way. No, there was no "probably" about it, Dylan amended silently. It was far better if they both pretended they were strangers.

"I'll be back when my shift is up." He was already heading toward the door before he stopped, his hand on the doorknob. "Want me to pick up anything on the way back?"

Lucy pressed her lips together. The question had all the feel of a domestic situation, as if they were playing house together. But they weren't and they wouldn't. The sooner she convinced herself of that, the better for all concerned, including her baby. Dylan had made it perfectly clear when he'd left her all those long months ago that he was not in it for the long haul, that he could never be in any relationship for the long haul, and that was the end of it.

There was no sense in her hoping for anything else. She wasn't a fool.

"No." She forced out the word as brightly as she could. "Unless they robbed the refrigerator, I think I have everything I need."

He nodded. "Get some rest. If you need anything, the detective's name outside is Reed."

Her mouth quirked. "What's his name inside?"

"What?"

She waved it away. "Never mind. Poor joke. Is Reed his first or last name?"

Only she would ask that. She'd always seemed bent on knowing everyone in the world on a first-name basis, while he had always wanted to hold everyone at arm's length. With her his arms hadn't been nearly long enough.

"Last." Dylan paused, knowing what she was waiting for. "His first name's Cameron." Pulling open the door, he turned to give her one last instruction. "Don't open the door to anyone you don't know."

An amused smile moved along her lips. She supposed, in his own way, he did care. Or maybe that was just the cop in him. "Yes, sir. And Dylan?"

Braced, he had no idea what was coming next. "Yes?" He watched as her pleasant smile turned almost beatific.

"Thank you."

Each time she thanked him, he felt more like a heel. And more convinced than ever that he had done the right thing. For her. "Yeah."

Lucy remained rooted to the spot, looking at the door he closed after himself as he left. *Same old Dylan.* The baby began to suck on her blouse, creating a spreading damp spot in its wake. Drawing it out of her mouth, Lucy looked down at the tiny, protesting face.

"So, what do you think of him so far?" The response came as Elena began to cry in earnest now. Lucy cuddled the baby to her. ''Yes, he can have that effect on you.'' She retreated to her bedroom.

It was time to feed her baby. Hers and Dylan's.

When Dylan returned from his shift, a shift that had been as unproductive as the others had been, several hours had gone by. The make of the car parked across the street from Lucy's house had changed. The sight of it pulled him up short.

It took Dylan a minute to place it. Kane Madigan's minivan.

The way the man's family was increasing, Dylan could readily see the need for one. What was more difficult to reconcile was that it was Kane who'd needed it. Kane, who had been such a loner. It was beginning to feel as if everyone with the Bedford Detective squad was a family man. Dylan was probably the last holdout.

That was the way he felt sometimes, like a holdout. Knowingly barricading himself away from happiness and a rich, full life. At least far richer than the one he had now.

But that rich, full life was only available to him in his dreams. Reality was different. Reality had husbands beating their wives and locking their children in dark closets, threatening to strip the skin from their bodies and beat them raw if they so much as whimpered. That was the sort of reality, the sort of heritage he had to deal with. It wasn't one he intended to pass on.

Dylan could have sworn he saw a grin on Kane's face when their eyes met. The other man gave him a two-fingered salute and started up his vehicle. The grin was no doubt directed his way because of the flowers he was carrying. Carnations. Pink ones.

Self-consciousness washed over him and he squelched the desire to hide the bouquet behind his back. Too late for that, anyway.

He threw a careless half shrug in Kane's direction. The detective wasn't looking his way any longer. He was apparently anxious to get home.

Dylan couldn't help wondering how that felt.

He knocked rather than opened the door the way he had the last two times. He didn't want to startle Lucy. But when she didn't come to answer the door within a couple of minutes, impatience and concern had Dylan resorting to his previous method of entry.

Tucking the bouquet under his arm, he almost had the door unlocked with his skeleton key when it was suddenly opened from inside.

"Sorry, I was just putting the baby—"

Lucy stopped abruptly as she saw the half-squashed flowers under his arm.

Annoyed, Dylan strode in. "Why didn't you ask who it was?" Didn't she know any better than to just unlock the door that way?

He was snapping at her again. It made her think of a tethered animal, snapping at passersby to keep them away. "Because I knew that if you were somebody dangerous, Kane would have stopped you by now."

He hadn't mentioned to her who would be relieving Reed. "You know Madigan?"

She nodded, wondering how long he was going to keep the flowers tucked under his arm. "He introduced himself when I went out to bring him coffee.''

She'd brought the man coffee. Dylan scowled at her. ''You're supposed to be resting.''

She did her best to ignore the fact that he was behaving like a wounded bear. ''Hard to rest when I know I'm under surveillance.''

She'd done something to her hair, he thought. Tied it on her head in a jaunty fashion that had curls cascading haphazardly around her face. Making his fingers itch to pull the pins out just to see it fall again. He tried to keep his mind on what he was saying.

''You're not under surveillance, you're just being looked after.''

''Whatever you say.'' Her eyes strayed from his face to the flowers getting progressively flatter under his arm. ''Are those for me?''

Dylan's eyebrows narrowed. Now, what was she talking about? ''What?''

''The flowers you're pressing against your side.'' She nodded at them. ''You know,'' Lucy deadpanned, ''you'd probably have more luck doing that if you dried them out first.''

Remembering, Dylan felt like a fool. ''Oh, yeah. These are for you.'' Clutching at the stems, wishing he hadn't bothered to bring the flowers in the first place, he shook them a little, as if they were crumpled-up clothes whose wrinkles needed to be shaken out. A few petals rained down on the rug like plump pink drops.

She took them, feeling the strange sting of tears starting. ''You remembered.''

He felt as if he were under a microscope. To his

recollection, she was the only human being who'd ever been able to make him feel that way. Usually, he just moved through life without thought to his actions or the repercussions they had. He certainly never felt awkward about it.

"Pink's not a hard color to remember. I thought maybe, under the circumstances, you might need a little welcome-home present."

Taking the flowers, she brought them into the kitchen. There was a vase in one of the lower cabinets. When pressed into service, it usually housed flowers that she bought herself.

"Your cleaning up the place did that." He'd done his best, but a closer survey had shown her that he hadn't been able to restore everything to its proper place the way she first thought. "By the way, it's usually easier if the kitchen towels are in the kitchen instead of the linen closet."

He couldn't really tell the difference between towels that belonged in the kitchen and those that belonged in the bathroom. "I don't have any towels in the kitchen."

That's right, she recalled. Dylan used paper towels. Keeping everything as disposable as possible in his life.

Filling the vase, she turned to look at him. "Yes, I remember."

For a second, she buried her face in the bouquet and inhaled deeply. Her gratitude was in her eyes when she raised them to his. But along with the gratitude was confusion.

"Dylan, I just don't know what to make of you."

"Then don't try." He glanced toward the bedroom. "How's the baby?"

She carried the vase to the dining room and placed it on the table. The whole room brightened. Or was that her smile? He wasn't sure.

"Sleeping like one, from the sound of it." She'd just put Elena down and was hoping for a couple of hours of respite. "Are you hungry?"

Yes, he was hungry, hungry for things he couldn't have, hungry for things that weren't meant for him. His mistake was in allowing himself to sample them once and temporarily lose his grip on reality. Dylan deliberately kept his distance from her.

"I ate something at the stakeout."

She cocked her head, amused. His answer had a familiar ring to it. "What?"

"I don't remember."

As she recalled, Dylan rarely remembered what he ate. That made his build that much more remarkable. "I thought as much. C'mon, I've got a pot roast ready. You can invite Kane in for some, too."

He found himself following her like a stray puppy, knowing he was treading on dangerous ground. The less that was exchanged between them, except for information pertaining to Ritchie, the better.

"Kane's gone home."

"Good, that's where he belongs." She opened the lower oven door and began to ease the roast from the rung. "He has a nice family."

Dylan elbowed her aside, taking the pot holders from her. She wasn't supposed to lift anything heavy. Even he knew that. What made her so damn stubborn? "How would you...?"

She indicated the counter, then moved the carving board beside the roast. Knowing better than to argue with him, she surrendered the large serving fork and waited until he lifted the roast from the pot and placed it on the board. "He showed me pictures."

Never the gregarious type, Kane had gotten noticeably friendlier since his marriage. Still, the man had had a reputation as being almost a loner.

"You're kidding."

But even as he commented, Dylan understood why Kane would have shown her photographs of his family. Outside of normal pride that would have prompted the display, there was the fact that Lucy was the type of woman people broke rules for. The type of woman people wanted to be close to. It was a little like sidling up to sunshine in human form. She had that way about her.

Without knowing she'd done it, she'd caused Dylan to bend a few rules himself. Rules he had once believed were cast in iron. Rules meant to preserve him as well as her. It had taken almost superhuman effort for him to adhere to them again once that initial discovery had been made.

But he knew what would happen if he thumbed his nose at them. Or pretended they no longer applied.

With an expert hand, she began to carve slices from the roast. "No, I'm not kidding. He wanted to show me his family. His wife is a knockout and those girls of his are adorable. He's hoping for a son, though, this time."

Dylan felt his jaw slacken. "This time? You mean she's…?"

He could only shake his head. Lucy's talents were wasted at her present job. The department would do well to have her carry on interrogations for them.

The unspoken word was understood. Placing two more slices on top of the two she'd already put on his plate, Lucy nodded.

"Just. They couldn't be happier." *Unlike the way you would have been if I'd told you,* she thought. She surrounded the slices with potatoes and carrots. Lucy moved his dish toward him. "C'mon," she coaxed, "the pot roast is getting cold."

Dylan looked down at the plate before him. It had been a long time since he'd faced a regular meal. "You did all this?"

"Putting a round piece of meat into a pot with a few vegetables isn't exactly equal to a seven-course dinner for twelve," she pointed out. Taking her own plate, she led the way into the dining room. She sat down at one end, leaving the other for him. The flowers were between them. "Besides, Sheila said I have to keep my strength up for the baby's sake."

He sat down at the other end. "Sheila?"

"My doctor."

"Right. And she is—right," he repeated. Taking refuge in eating, he managed several bites before stopping.

Lucy raised her eyes to his. He wasn't eating. "Something wrong?"

Everything was wrong, he thought, and it had been ever since he'd heard Alexander say Ritchie's name. If Alexander and Hathaway had taken their discussion elsewhere, or if he'd been out just then, none of this would be going on.

But it was, and there were responsibilities to face, no matter how unpleasant. "The funeral's tomorrow."

Her appetite, not strong to begin with, disappeared entirely. She sat staring at her food. "I know."

She shouldn't have to go through this so soon after having a baby, he thought. "I don't think that you—"

She anticipated him. The sad look vanished, replaced by a determined one.

"I'm going. I'm not some fragile piece of china, Dylan. And he was my brother. My only family except for Elena." She wasn't going to let herself cry. If she cried, she was going to fall to pieces and that was a luxury she didn't have. Not even alone in her room.

He wanted to ask about the baby's father again, but he banked down the urge, not wanting to upset her any more than she already was.

"All right." He moved the vase to one side, wanting to see her face and gauge her reaction. "Mind if I go with you?"

She hadn't known if he was going to attend or not. With Dylan, there were no assumptions. He was kind when she thought he would be cruel and cruel when she thought he would be kind. Lucy nodded, smiling. "Ritchie would have liked that."

It wasn't Ritchie he was thinking of right now. "Yeah."

Lucy paused in the living room, the blanket draped over her arm. Dylan was making a place for himself on the sofa. "You can have Ritchie's old room, you know. The baby's staying in my room for the time being."

He tucked a sheet carelessly into the cushions. "Being out here is more sensible."

Shaking her head, she tucked the sheet in further, smoothing out what he had done. "You always were that. Sensible."

Her arm brushed against his as he moved back. Dylan looked at her for a long moment. "Oh, I don't know about that."

She knew she should have left it alone. Just left the blanket where it was, turned around and gone to bed, shutting the door on him. But she hadn't been able to successfully do that in nine months. What made her think she could do it now?

"Was being with me so insensible?"

It had been the most wonderful part of his life, but it hadn't been sensible. They both knew that. There was no point in restating it. "It's been a long day for you, Lucy. Go to bed."

She felt as if she were being dismissed. Like a child. But she didn't hurt like a child, she hurt like a full-grown woman.

Lucy clenched her hands at her sides, wanting to say something to him, wanting to shake him the way he'd shaken her. But what good would it do? They'd said their goodbyes nine months ago. And flowers or not, nothing had happened to change that.

"Good night, then."

He watched her leave, wishing the sight of her walking away didn't cut through him the way it did.

Chapter 7

The digital clock on the mantel announced in red, luminous numbers that it was 3:07 as Lucy crept quietly into the living room. She wasn't accustomed to moving so slowly, but she didn't want to make any noise and wake Dylan up. If he actually was asleep. If he wasn't, she didn't want to call his attention to her. She intended to ease out of the room before he noticed her.

Elena was back in her crib after a lengthy feeding. Nighttime was the hardest. The infant would fall asleep, nursing, only to wake up once her source of milk was taken away. But she had finally had her fill and fallen asleep in earnest.

Which was more than Lucy could do. Awake and restless, acutely conscious of the man who was only a few rooms away, Lucy found herself wondering if he was really asleep. It had been a long time since she had seen him sleeping.

Softly, Lucy crossed the threshold into the room, her eyes focused on the inert figure lying on the sofa. His eyes were shut.

The blanket she'd given him was bunched up at his feet and the pillow was only partially under his head. He'd always been a restless sleeper, she remembered, a fond smile tugging at her lips.

What do I make of you, Dylan McMorrow? Why are you back in my life now, when I'm trying so hard to get it all in order? So hard to get over you? Will I never be free of you?

She knew the answer to that.

Seeing him again, seeing him here, only told her what she had always known deep in her heart. That, even though she'd accepted they'd never be together again, she would always love him.

Who said you got wiser with age? she mused. She certainly hadn't.

But maybe it took more than nine months to get over someone like Dylan McMorrow. A brooding man of mystery who could be so kind when he wanted to be. And so cruel when he didn't realize it.

And maybe holding his daughter in her arms, seeing Dylan's intense dark blue eyes looking up at her from Elena's face, didn't help things along, either.

A sigh escaped her lips as she drew closer. The blanket that only moments before had been bunched up at his feet was now lying in a heap on the floor beside the sofa. Shaking her head, her eyes on his sleeping face, she bent down and picked it up. For a split second, she debated covering him with it. There was a slight early-morning chill lingering in the room, but it probably wasn't enough to affect him. The man radiated heat; he didn't need a blanket over him.

She took a step back, holding the blanket to her. Telling herself she was only imagining the scent of that musky cologne he always wore clinging to it. Shadows caused by the street lamp outside the window played across his face the way she longed to. Asleep, his face at rest, Dylan didn't look nearly as brooding as he did when awake.

He looked, she thought, like the man she'd fallen in love with. That gentle soul hidden deep within a sharp, pointy shell that he'd erected so that the world would think twice before getting in his way. So it would think twice before hurting him.

At least that was what she'd told herself she saw there.

Probably all just hallucination on her part. Pressing her lips together, calling herself a hopeless fool, Lucy turned away and crossed the room to the doorway.

"Can't you wait until I'm up before you start making up my bed?"

Almost out of the room, Lucy froze in place. She should have realized he wasn't asleep. He'd been too still. Asleep, he always tossed and turned. And besides, now that she thought about it, Dylan always slept with what amounted to having one eye open. Wary. Always wary. She figured it was the cop in him.

Turning around again, Lucy glanced down self-consciously at the blanket in her hands. "I was just checking on you."

He sat up, still looking at her. Was that the real

reason she'd come out looking for him? Or had she lain in her bed, wanting him as much as he wanted her?

More than likely, the break-in was just making her nervous. Nighttime had a way of magnifying even the smallest of fears. He could bear witness to that. His voice rumbled to her across the room. "I'm still here."

"I knew you would be. I just..." How could she put into words what she didn't really understand herself? He'd made it clear that he didn't want her before he left. What was she doing, standing here like some misguided rock singer's groupie, staring at him in the semidark?

With a half shrug, she looked over her shoulder toward the doorway. "I'd better get back to bed."

"Good idea."

The hurt came, fresh and new, even though she told herself she was being an idiot and he wasn't supposed to be able to hurt her anymore. With an inclination of her head in his direction, she turned away.

About to lie down again, Dylan watched her retreat. As she came to the threshold, the light from the hall mingled with the fibers of her white nightgown, turning it into translucent gauze.

Turning his mouth into cotton and driving a hard fist into the pit of his stomach.

When she turned around to look at him one last time, the light illuminating her body, reminding him of everything he'd given away, his breath caught in his throat, threatening to strangle him.

"I didn't mean to wake you."

"You didn't." He managed to bite the words off,

struggling with feelings he had thought he'd buried. "Go to bed, Lucy. Go to bed before…"

The room was dark except for the light coming in through the window, but she could have sworn she saw desire in his eyes. Just for a second. She felt it flash through her own body.

"Before what?"

"Before you run out of time." He nodded toward the clock on the mantel. "The funeral's at eight."

"Yes, I know," she said quietly, then turned away and left the room.

He didn't sleep the rest of the night.

At five, he made his way into the kitchen to make coffee. He heard water running and realized she had to be taking a shower. The mental image that flashed across his mind almost drove him crazy. They had taken a shower together once, and he had made her stand perfectly still while he soaped her body. Halfway through he had broken down and made love to her with the water running in both their faces.

He swore and wished for a cigarette. Or a strong shot of whiskey, then laughed at himself when he saw the time. Strong coffee was going to have to do.

To distract himself, he called Watley to remind him that he was attending the funeral and was going to be late taking his turn at the stakeout.

The voice that answered the phone on the other end was groggy, and far from friendly. "Damn it, McMorrow, did your ugly mug stop all the clocks where you are? Why the hell did you have to wake me up at 5:00 a.m. to tell me something you already told me?''

''Just making sure you remember.'' The sound of running water finally stopped. Dylan exhaled a long breath.

''At 5:00 a.m. I'm lucky if I remember my own name. Do me a favor. No more pop quizzes until at least eight, okay?''

Dylan laughed shortly. ''You sleep too much.''

''Sorry, Count Dracula, we can't all keep your hours. Can I go now?'' Watley mumbled sleepily.

''Yeah.'' Dylan heard fumbling in the background as Watley undoubtedly searched for the receiver's cradle. The connection was broken.

Dylan drained his cup, forcing himself to remain where he was until Lucy came out to join him. When she did, he struggled to look disinterested. There was no point in letting her know his thoughts kept centering around her.

She had on a simple T-shirt and jeans that clung as tightly to her body as he wished he were free to. Beads of water clung to a few strands of hair just around her face and she looked agitated.

Despite his pledge to keep distant, he felt his sympathy aroused. ''Nervous?''

''No.'' She took a deep breath, then looked at him, relenting. ''Yes.''

''If you don't feel up to going—''

''That's not up for debate,'' she said firmly. Needing something to do, she crossed to the refrigerator. ''Can I make you breakfast?''

''I don't eat breakfast.''

She shut the door again. ''That's right, I remember.''

He watched her move away from the refrigerator. "Doesn't mean you can't."

But she shook her head. Her stomach was already in a tight knot. The thought of food only made it worse. "Not unless you want me throwing up on you."

She shouldn't have to be going through this. "Lucy—"

But she waved him back before he could get started. "I'm fine," she snapped, then felt ashamed. Her voice softened. "There's just this huge knot in my stomach right now." She picked up the coffee-pot and began to pour herself a cup. Coffee she could always use. Her hand shook.

He saw and took the pot from her, finishing the job. Dylan passed the cup to her. "What about the baby?"

She took it in both hands, easing herself onto a kitchen stool. "I have someone coming to watch her."

His eyebrows drew together. He trusted no one, especially not now. "Who?"

"One of the girls I have working in my shop." She noticed his expression and smiled. "Don't worry, she's reliable."

He supposed it would be all right. He didn't like leaving the baby alone in the house with only a teenager for protection, but he'd arranged for Reed to return this morning to watch the house. That should take care of any problems.

"Looks like you've got things covered," he murmured. He poured himself a second cup, avoiding her eyes and what looking at them did to him.

* * *

Her fingers dug into his flesh. Dylan didn't even remember taking her hand. Instinct must have prompted him. The same instinct that told him Lucy needed all the support he could give her. The strong face she turned toward the world was still there, still intact, but the rest of the world didn't know her the way he did. Inside, she was all in pieces. All her life, she had been very close to her brother. In the beginning, he had been her mentor, her idol. Gradually, that had changed and maybe even reversed a little. Ritchie might have been the older one, but it was Lucy who had been the stable one. The only thing that never changed was the way she felt about him. She had always doted on Ritchie.

Dylan remembered envying what they had as a family. And envying the absolute strength of the love that Lucy bore for her brother. Love had never really been a part of his own life. Oh, his mother had tried in her own way, and he had felt protective of her, but it hadn't been love in any real sense of the word. A woman who loved her child didn't allow herself and her child to be abused time and again.

Word of Ritchie's death had spread. A large number of his friends turned out to attend the service and to follow the hearse to the cemetery, where they paid their last respects as the casket was lowered into the ground.

Standing at the grave site, Dylan looked around. He didn't recognize most of the people there. Without asking, he knew that these were people on the fringes of a world Dylan had sworn to keep apart from the normal, law-abiding one.

But he did recognize the man who approached

Lucy right after the priest had concluded his service and said a few last words to her.

The man, who carried himself as if he were taller than just average height, had silver-gray hair and a thin face. The suit he had on probably cost more than the combined tab for the clothes of every other person there.

Alfred Palmero. The owner of Den of Thieves. Even the name seemed to thumb its nose at the police. Yet here he was, acting the part of the saddened employer, coming toward Lucy with hands outstretched, every nail perfectly manicured and buffed.

In the melodic voice that led the church choir and could have belonged to a tenor in an opera, Palmero greeted Lucy and enveloped Lucy in a deep embrace before she saw the latter coming. Gray-blue eyes that could only be described as flinty passed fleetingly over Dylan, appraising him instantly and finding him lacking, before returning to Lucy. A respectful two steps behind him was a man who acted as his chauffeur and doubled as his bodyguard.

"Such a sad, sad day." Ending the embrace, he took possession of both of her hands in his. "Oh, my dear Lucy, I just want you to know how deeply sorry I am about your brother. Ritchie was far too young and vital a man to be taken from us so abruptly, so cruelly. We all liked him at the restaurant and we are all going to miss him a great deal." Sympathy seemed to spill from every pore. He lowered his voice, as if to exclude even her companion. "I know this is a particularly rough time for you, especially with the baby and all. If there is anything

I can do for you, all you have to do is let me know.'' His eyes washed over her, approval evident in the scrutiny. ''Anything,'' he repeated softly. ''A job, a loan—''

Lucy raised her chin, removing her hands from his like a regal queen suffering the touch of a commoner solely out of the goodness of her heart. Charity of the pocket was something she never expected and never accepted. All she ever required was charity of the soul and she didn't see it in Palmero's eyes.

''Thank you, but I'm fine.'' Things were a little tight, but it went that way at times. She had years of experience to fall back on when it came to that. As a teenager, she'd worked at the card and gift store she now owned. Tight times passed and better times came as long as you hung on. It was that way with everything.

It had been her fondest hope that Ritchie would someday work at the shop as well so that she could keep an eye on him. Now that wasn't going to happen.

She couldn't think about that now.

Lucy felt Dylan move a little closer to her. He was being protective of her. It reinforced her resolve. Her eyes met Palmero's. ''I'm sure I won't be bothering you.''

''Absolutely no bother at all,'' Palmero assured her. ''Trust me.''

It occurred to Lucy that the serpent in the Garden of Eden could have hissed the same words in the exactly the same manner to Eve just before he pushed the apple on her. Though dapper and almost fastidiously stylish, her brother's former employer made her think of a snake toying with its prey.

"I hope I never need to," she told him before turning to Dylan. "I'd like to go home, please." He gave her his arm and she slipped her hand through it. "Goodbye, Mr. Palmero. Thank you for your good wishes. I'm sure they would have meant a lot to Ritchie."

The silver head inclined, acknowledging her words. "Goodbye, my dear. I'll be in touch."

She wasn't sure whether or not Dylan was right in his estimation of Palmero's connection to Ritchie's death, but that wasn't the kind of thing Dylan would have made up. Dylan wasn't given to lies. And if he was right...

"Is it just me," she whispered to Dylan as they began walking away, "or do you suddenly feel the need for a shower, too?"

She was sharp, Dylan thought, not without a small touch of pride though he knew he had no right to the feeling. A great many people had been deceived by Palmero and his polished manners. "I see you weren't taken in."

She looked at him in surprise. Didn't he know her at all? Just because she was upset didn't mean she'd suddenly become stupid. "I've become a great deal more cynical since you walked away." She saw that her words had made a direct hit, but the victory felt hollow. She changed the subject. "Why would Palmero come to Ritchie's funeral? Ritchie only worked for him a short while."

Opening the passenger door, he helped Lucy into the car. "Maybe he just wants to oil his way into your confidence.'' He closed her door and rounded the hood of the car.

She shifted toward Dylan as he got in. ''Then I'm afraid he's going to need more oil than a full-size tanker can carry. I just don't like the man.''

Dylan laughed and the sound warmed her. It helped to quell the ache she felt in her heart. Saying goodbye to Ritchie had been even harder than she'd anticipated. It was all she could do to keep the tears under control.

The knock on her window made her jerk. A smile slipped into place when she saw it was Alma. Lucy pressed the button to roll down the window.

''You going to be okay, kid?'' Showing concern, Alma's eyes slanted toward Dylan's profile as she asked her question.

Lucy smiled. Less than three months separated them, but Alma had always insisted on calling her kid. ''Yes. I'll be in the store—''

''In a month,'' Alma told her sharply. ''There's nothing there that needs your attention. I've got Beth and Margaret taking turns coming in, though it always seems like the same person.'' To Alma, the twin teenagers were utterly interchangeable. ''And I can handle the receipts until the doctor says you're ready to come in.''

''Alma, I'm fine,'' Lucy protested. Why did everyone insist on treating her as if she was some mindless, frail little thing? Didn't anyone realize that she needed to be busy, to keep her mind busy until she could make peace with what had happened?

''The doctor, not you,'' Alma emphasized. She leaned into the car, raising her voice. ''And you, stone face..." Dylan turned to look at her. "You see she gets her rest, or I'll come after you."

For the first time since he'd walked back into her life, laughter bubbled in Lucy's throat. She stifled it, but it took effort.

Dylan merely inclined his head in silent acquiescence, waiting for Alma to withdraw. When she finally did, after first giving Lucy's hand a quick squeeze, Dylan started up the car and pulled out of the parking lot.

"Alma still has that winning personality, I see."

Lucy turned back in her seat after waving goodbye. "Alma worries about me."

Barely avoiding being sideswiped by a blue sports car determined to beat the light, Dylan gripped the steering wheel a little harder than he might have normally. "She's not the only one."

Lucy paused, considering. "I don't think Palmero was worried as much as—"

Dylan spared her a glance as he slowed down for the next light. "I wasn't talking about Palmero."

"Then who?" Puzzled, she looked at him. There were lines around his mouth and that furrow along his brow, giving her the answer. "You?" When he said nothing, she thought of dropping it, then decided to push it instead. "You know, it wouldn't hurt you to say yes."

"Yes."

The response was abject, lifeless. As if he were answering a routine survey that had no claim to his attention. Why was admitting to being concerned about her so hard for him? "Yes like you mean it."

"Yes like I mean it," he deadpanned.

Lucy laughed, shaking her head. "What are we doing here?"

He kept his eyes on the road, thinking it simpler that way. She had a way of distracting him. "I'm driving you home."

"No," she persisted, "I mean what are we *doing* here? You, me, this invisible waltz we're dancing, what's it all about?"

She couldn't quite read the look he sent her way, but there was a tinge of exasperation about it.

"Alma was right. You need to rest. This was hard on you."

He was taking refuge in routines, in words and denial. She sighed and leaned back in the seat. She had to be out of her mind, trying to get something out of him. Thinking that if she just said the right thing, pressed the right buttons, she'd finally get some sort of show of feelings from him. You couldn't get blood out of a stone, or even water for that matter. A stone was what it was. A stone, nothing more, nothing less. Stones were the kind of thing walls were made of, not bridges.

Still, she couldn't help herself. Maybe her emotions were more raw than she thought. "And you? How about you? Was this hard on you, seeing Ritchie buried, or was everything I ever thought about you wrong? Don't you care about anyone?"

Her words stung, surprising him. As far as upbraidings went, he'd certainly been subjected to worse. Hardened to worse. And yet, the sound of her voice cracking undid him the way a tongue-lashing heaped with vile names couldn't have.

"Yeah, it was hard on me," he admitted quietly, still keeping his eyes on the road. "Ritchie and I go way back. He could always make me laugh even when there wasn't anything funny to laugh at.'' His mouth curved just a little as he remembered. ''He always got such a damn big kick out of life. I thought he was crazy.''

''I thought he was right. You're supposed to enjoy life.''

''Maybe he enjoyed it a little to much,'' Dylan commented. ''And forgot about the hard-work part. I guess he left that to you.''

''He had a little growing to do,'' she allowed, then realized she was still doing what she'd always done. She was defending her brother. He wasn't going to need her defending him any longer.

Pressing her lips together again, she turned her face away from Dylan's. Tears were coming again and she didn't want him to see them.

Without a word, Dylan pulled up a tissue from the small dispenser straddling the bucket seat partition and handed it to her. He kept his eyes on the road as she took it from him. She didn't say anything. She didn't have to. Some things were just understood.

''Well?''

Palmero shrugged out of his expensive jacket and hung it meticulously on the hanger before easing it into the closet, where he made sure it wasn't near anything else. He liked his clothes without a hint of wrinkles.

''She's either completely in the dark about the tape, or one hell of a cool customer.''

The man behind the desk frowned, disturbed. ''Never met a woman who could tell the truth yet.''

Plunging his hand into a candy dish, he caught up a fistful of mints and tossed some of them into his mouth. "My guess is that she has it hidden someplace."

Palmero kept the disdain out of his voice. The man behind the desk was his superior and the rank demanded respect even if the man didn't. "Where? We tore up her house."

"A safety deposit box?" he asked as he chewed.

Palmero shook. "No keys, no bank statements to indicate that any box exists."

The other man tossed back what was left of his cache. When he spoke, irritation vibrated in his voice. "Maybe she's got it hidden at work. Find out where she works."

The sneer on Palmero's lips was condescending. "Already taken care of. It's a card-and-gift shop at Ballenger and Havard. I've got someone there now." He glanced at his watch. The job should be finished by now. "If the tape's there, we'll find it."

The other man's eyes narrowed. Satisfied, he took another handful of mints. His eyes disappeared into slits as a smile took over his mouth.

"Good work."

Chapter 8

Dylan hesitated, his hand on the doorknob. Inside of him, there was a battle going on. He wanted to leave, but he was unwilling to close the door behind him, shutting Lucy out. Not when there was so much for her to deal with all at once.

The girl from the card shop was still here watching Elena, and he'd seen another one of the off-duty detectives in a car across the street, but he still thought of Lucy as being alone.

He sighed, turning from the door, knowing he was going to regret this.

She looked worn, he thought. Beautiful, but worn. No one ever filled him with ambivalent feelings the way Lucy did.

He looked for the right words. When they didn't come, he asked, ''You sure you'll be all right?''

That he even asked told her that there were at least some feelings left between them. Or maybe, she amended, it was the public servant in him that was asking.

The thought almost made her smile. If there was anyone who the label "servant" didn't begin to fit, it was Dylan.

She bit her lower lip, as if she was actually thinking about his question, then raised her chin that way he'd seen her do so many times before. That way that said she wasn't about to let the world roll over on her. "I'll have to be, won't I?"

The pragmatic answer wasn't quite like her. The fire was missing. But then, there'd been a lot going on to extinguish it, not the least of which was apparently being abandoned by the father of her child. Duty silently warred with a sense of responsibility he'd long since told himself wasn't his.

Dylan looked over her shoulder. "I could stay for a while."

She knew where he was looking. At the clock on the mantel. He wasn't anyone's servant, but he was conscious of responsibilities and she was keeping him from his.

"But then you'd have to leave eventually and I'd still be alone." She moved toward him, ready to usher him out the door. Something akin to tenderness stirred within her. She figured when it came to Dylan, it always would. "Go, Dylan. Go to work. Go do what you're good at." She looked around the room, trying to lose herself in small details to keep the larger ones from assaulting her. "I can manage here. Since Alma won't let me set foot in the store, I might even decide to repaint the house." She smiled up at him. "What's your favorite color these days?"

He looked at her, feeling himself being pulled in all directions at once. ''Blue.''

''Blue.'' Lucy shook her head. He'd said the word as if he were a stone statue come to life. She placed her hand on his arm, as if to coax or shake something more out. ''C'mon, Dylan, even you can do better than that. Elaborate a little. Dark blue, light blue, electric-blue, blue-gray, blue-green, turquoise, what?''

''Blue,'' he repeated. And then he added, ''Dark, like your eyes.''

For just a moment, the past and most of the present disappeared. The air and her heart stood still. ''I didn't think you even noticed that.''

Without being completely conscious of what he was doing, he cupped his hand along her cheek. It was as soft as he remembered. Maybe softer. ''Hard not to when they're looking right into me.''

She felt each one of his fingers burn into her skin and told herself she didn't notice. ''Maybe that's just your guilty conscience.''

Dylan didn't bother denying it. What was the point? ''Maybe.''

When he tried to reconstruct it in his mind later, he wasn't sure if he had been the one who made the first move or not. Probably. Lucy was far too proud a woman to venture any further than she already had.

All he really knew for sure was that what happened took place in a haze. One moment, he was looking into those quicksilver-blue eyes of hers, losing his way, and the next, he found his hands tangled in her hair, his fingers cupping the back of her head. And his mouth kissing her with all the passion that had been bottled up inside of him for all these long months. Kissing her as his blood surged and pounded through his body, mocking him and telling him that he'd been a fool to have ever turned his back on someone like Lucy.

The instant she felt his breath on her lips, felt him touch his mouth to hers, her head began to spin. She didn't want to give in, didn't want to let the kiss be anything more than an aberration of time and space, didn't want it taking all of her good sense.

Sense had little to do with the feelings that came running out of hiding the moment Dylan began to lower his head toward hers. If she'd had any sense at all, she would have turned her head away.

But she didn't.

She had a crying need to feel his mouth on hers again, to savor the feeling and the flavor one more moment and seal it to her.

"I'm not the kind who makes promises, Lucy, just prophesies."

"Oh, and what's your prophesy for me?"

"That I'll hurt you."

"I'll take my chances."

And she had, she thought now, remembering his warning when things had heated up between them. She'd taken her chances and she'd lost. But for one second, she'd revisit what had brought her to this juncture in her life. What had caused her to leave her strict upbringing behind and give herself to a man who'd told her that nothing permanent could ever be between them.

He'd lied. There was something permanent.

There was Elena, and no matter what happened, she would always be grateful to him for that.

When her body leaned into his, so softly, so willingly, temptation reared its head, whispering words into his ear. Urging him to forget everything but the woman in his arms and the moment he'd seized.

Dylan normally regarded his cell phone as an annoying nuisance he was forced to carry with him because of his job. But when it rang now, he thought of it as an ally, offering him a way out. Before he allowed himself to do something Lucy would live to regret.

Because he couldn't give her any more now than he could before.

Lucy drew her head back, fighting for focus. Struggling to gather her senses together. She nodded toward his jacket. "Unless your jacket has suddenly decided to break into a musical number, I think your phone is ringing."

He frowned, at himself, at his own weakness, and at Watley in absentia because the latter had reprogrammed his telephone not to ring, but to chime. The first eleven notes of the "Sound of Music" replayed themselves when he didn't answer. He'd yet to get it reprogrammed and Watley had sworn he'd lost the instructions.

Dragging his hand through his hair as he simultaneously dragged air back into his lungs and contemplated what he deemed as justifiable homicide, Dylan swore under his breath. He pulled out his cell phone, flipped it open and barked, "McMorrow."

There was a pause on the other end of the line, as if uncertain of the connection. And then he heard a woman's voice. It wasn't dispatch.

"McMorrow, this is Alma. They gave me your number at the station. I'm at the card shop. I think you should get over here right away. And don't—" But it was too late for her final instruction.

"Alma?" He couldn't begin to guess why a woman who hated his very shadow would be calling him on his cell phone. Or why her voice sounded so oddly shaky.

Lucy was immediately alert. "Alma?" She grabbed his arm, trying to hear what was being said on the other end of the line. "Why is Alma calling you?"

She heard Alma sigh. "I was going to tell you not to say anything to Lucy, but I see it's too late for that."

"Yeah." Lucy had managed to angle the phone so that she could hear, too. With very little effort he could twist his hand free. But to leave her in the dark wouldn't be fair. He knew how he would have felt in her position. "What's wrong?"

Alma's voice was deathly still. He'd been around enough victims to know she was struggling to keep her composure and not give in to fear. "Somebody broke into the store while I was gone."

"I'll be right there." Dylan flipped the phone closed. At the same moment, he saw the look on Lucy's face. "You're not coming with me."

Oh, yes she was, she thought. "We're still in tune a little, I see."

His eyes narrowed. There was no way he was going to take her with him.

"No, we're not, because if we were, you'd be able to read my mind right now and you wouldn't like what you found there." He turned from her and went to the door. When she matched him step for step, he swung around again. "Stay home, Lucy. Paint the house like you said."

She tried to look glib. Tried not to dwell on the fact that everything around her seemed to be coming apart. "Too late, lost the inspiration."

He bit back his temper and attempted to reason with her. "You've got a baby, remember? What if she wakes up and she's hungry?"

"Breast milk in the refrigerator. Beth will handle it."

He closed his eyes. Breast milk in a bottle. "Too much information."

She thought she detected a slight pink hue along his neck and cheeks. Maybe it was the lighting. And then again, maybe not. The thought that he was embarrassed amused her. "You asked."

Dylan caught her by the shoulders, curbing the urge to shake sense into her head. "Look, this isn't some Nancy Drew story, Lucy. Someone is after something. We don't know what, and we're not completely sure who."

He'd all but told her he was certain it was Palmero. "But you said—"

"Never mind what I said." Exasperation was evident in every word. "I don't want you getting in the way and getting hurt."

Her eyes held his. She wasn't going to be talked out of this. "Haven't you heard? I've developed very tough skin."

She was talking about them, about their past. Damn it, for two cents... "But it's not invulnerable—"

No, not invulnerable, she thought. He had seen

to that. "I'm working on it." Angry, Lucy shrugged him off, every inch the fighter. "Now, *you* look. It's my store. I worked my tail off to buy that shop. You can't keep me from going." And then, as if reading his thoughts, she smiled a little. "And tying me up would come under the heading of police brutality."

"More like police smarts," he muttered audibly. Scowling, he surrendered. "Okay, give your instructions to Beth and we'll go."

But instead of going to Beth, the way he'd hoped, Lucy raised her voice and called out to the girl, telling her to come into the living room. Waiting, Lucy glanced at him. "I'm not stupid, Dylan."

So much for making his getaway while she was in the other room. He should have known better. "No, no one ever accused you of that."

Only me, she thought.

The shop looked like an earthquake had hit it. The shelving that housed the greeting cards had been knocked over. The various figurines, fancy frames and stationery boxes were thrown from their perches to the floor. Christmas ornaments lay smashed and broken for the most part.

Alma had looked up sharply when Dylan and Lucy entered. Fury was in her brown eyes as the petite blonde crossed to them.

Lucy simply walked past her as if she was in a trance. "Why did you bring her here?" Alma demanded.

Dylan didn't take to being yelled at, but this once, he let Alma have some slack. He was annoyed with himself for the way things had arranged themselves. But kissing Lucy had stripped him of his ability to think and Alma's call had caught him with his guard down.

"I didn't have much choice in the matter."

Walking away, he conferred with the two uniformed policemen who'd already taken notes and were now in the process of taking pictures of the scene. But even though he was talking to the men, his attention remained focused on Lucy. From where he was, he could see her face was immobile, but he knew that wouldn't last. Lucy was not one to remain devoid of emotions for long. They were just gathering up a full head of steam.

He wanted to protect her. He wanted to send her home. This was no place for her.

Nodding his head at something one of the policemen said, he crossed to Lucy. She'd picked up a figure of an angel. The wings were broken off. Taking it from her hand, he put it aside on the counter. "This could just be a random break-in."

Suspicious, Alma pounced on the words. "Why wouldn't it be?"

That's right, Lucy thought. Alma didn't know. "Because he thinks that someone's looking for something," Lucy told her. The numbness she'd felt when she walked in to the shop was beginning to recede, supplanted by barely contained rage. The same people who had invaded her store had more than likely invaded her home. And her life by killing her brother. She wanted justice. For her brother and for herself. If that wasn't available, she wanted revenge. She looked at the only man who could help her get that. "Isn't that right, Dylan?"

"Looking for something?" Alma asked. "Looking for what? Discount coupons?'' She waved an angry hand at the shambles on the floor. ''They sifted through everything, absolutely everything. You should see the storeroom.''

The words were no sooner out of Alma's mouth than Lucy was hurrying to the back to see the damage in the storeroom for herself. Dylan was right behind her.

Opening the door, she took a breath and turned on the light. It illuminated a state of chaos. Within the small, airless room, towering boxes, once carefully piled one on top of the another, were now toppled, their sides ripped open, their insides spilled out all over the floor. Children's videos and audiocassettes of time-worn favorite songs, mingled with gift books, more cards and figurines of cheery-looking animals in a macabre dance that covered the entire area.

Lucy covered her mouth, not knowing how much more of this she could take. ''Oh, God.''

Dylan wanted to take her in his arms, to tell her everything was going to be all right. But he didn't make promises. He just kept his word, once given. Instead, he turned to Alma. He'd felt her eyes boring into the back of his neck like a laser beam.

''Was anything taken?''

One shoulder rose and fell in abject confusion. ''Damned if I know. It's going to take me hours of going over the inventory to find out. Besides, there's nothing of real value to take. There wasn't even money in the register—which they broke into, I might add. It looks like someone jimmied it apart.''

Leaving Lucy behind, Dylan walked out again

and looked at the cash register. It was on its side behind the counter, its drawer hanging open like a broken jaw. Whoever had done it had been thorough. Nothing was left untouched.

He turned around to find Alma right behind him. Lucy was just walking out of the storeroom, still looking stunned.

"Don't touch anything until we can get the forensics team out here." He'd placed a call to them while driving over to the shop, but they were busy with another crime scene and couldn't be over until later.

Alma clicked her heels at attention and saluted. "Yes, sir."

Lucy placed herself between her best friend and her former lover. She knew Alma was only acting this way out of loyalty to her. But it wouldn't accomplish anything and they had more important matters to deal with. She wanted to get her shop back on its feet as soon as possible. "Do you think they left any prints?"

Amateurs would have, but Dylan had a feeling these were no amateurs.

"It's doubtful. They didn't at your house," he pointed out. "But anything's possible." There was always a chance someone had gotten careless. They needed very little to start with.

Alma swung around to look at Lucy, horror and disbelief on her face.

"Your house? Someone broke into your house?" she demanded, her hands on Lucy's shoulders. "Why didn't you tell me?"

Lucy shrugged. "I didn't want to worry you." Alma began to open her mouth in protest, but Lucy raised her hand to stop her from saying anything. "Don't start with me, Alma. This hasn't exactly been the best day of my life." Struggling to hold on to her temper, she looked around again. The task looked almost hopeless from where she stood. But everything began with the first step. She needed to take it. "We need to call the insurance company first to cover our losses."

The bright side, she counseled herself. Look at the bright side. Right now, that was almost impossible to find, but she tried.

She looked at Alma. "We're going to have to sell all these at a discount."

Alma looked at her dubiously, then took in the area. "Sure, we can call it a break-in sale. Might even catch on."

Lucy laughed shortly. It was better than crying. "You think?"

There was just so much of this he could watch. Lucy was torturing herself. Dylan took her elbow. When she raised her eyes to his questioningly, he saw the pain.

"Why don't I take you back home?" It wasn't really a suggestion, it was a plan. "There's nothing you can do here until after forensics is finished. Might take the better part of the afternoon. Alma can handle things until the team leaves."

Lucy wanted to protest, to scream and rail at something. At him. To lash out just for lashing out's sake, but that would only drain her more and solve nothing. It wouldn't replace a single thing, wouldn't right a single stand. Dylan was right. There wasn't anything she could do right now.

And there was a baby back at home who needed

her. At least there she could be useful. Temporarily giving up the battle, she nodded.

"All right. For now."

"Now is all I'm working with," he told her.

Alma looked at Dylan. He'd broken her best friend's heart and for a rather well regarded police detective, he was as thick as mud when it came to the parentage of Lucy's baby. But at least he'd managed to talk her into going home. She gave him his due grudgingly. "I guess you're good for some things."

He made no answer as he followed Lucy out the door. It was better that way for all concerned.

"I'll call you later tonight," Alma promised, raising her voice as Lucy and Dylan left the store.

Lucy stopped in the doorway and waved, then turned toward Dylan once they were outside. "Don't pay any attention to Alma."

"Don't worry about that," he said. Because part of the street in front of the shop was being repaved, he'd parked on the other side. Taking her elbow, he waited to cross the street.

Feeling unsteady on her feet, she let him guide her to the car over the uneven road. "She doesn't like you because of what happened between us."

He didn't want to get into that. He didn't want to open doors that were best left shut. "No explanations necessary."

He was pretending nothing had ever happened between them. As if what had been there hadn't ever existed. Lucy felt the threads of her patience unraveling down to nothing.

"Oh, there're lots of explanations necessary," she said, her voice rising to a dangerous level as she got into his car. "But that's your answer to everything, right? If it's not a case, you don't want to hear about it, talk about it, nothing. All you want to do is just shut it out of your mind."

Starting the car, he backed out of the spot and then turned it around to head back to her house. "Lucy—"

But his words had unleashed her pent-up feelings. She wasn't going to let him ignore their past. It existed. And because of it, Elena existed. "Because if it's not a case, then it doesn't deserve your attention. You even cut Ritchie out of your life so you wouldn't have to talk about why you walked out on everything between us."

Her voice was quavering, making him uneasy. He didn't know how to deal with tears, never had. Not his mother's and not hers. "Lucy—"

"The only reason you're interested in him now is because he's a homicide to you, so that means you have to play policeman and pretend you're actually a living, breathing human being instead of some machine that—" Her voice hitched. "Some machine that—"

Lucy's voice broke completely. Tears filled her eyes, spilling out into her soul. Seeping through eyelids that were pressed shut.

He heard them and they tore at him, frustrating him. He had no idea what to do, how to make her stop. "Lucy—"

Turning her head away, she waved a dismissive hand at him. She was angry with herself for crying in front of him this way. She should have been braver. More controlled, the way he was. He didn't give a damn about anything except his work.

Frustrated, Dylan pulled his car over to the side of the road. There were things he wanted to say to her, things he suddenly wanted to explain. But no words came, nothing formed in his mind. He'd never been good at talking. People hadn't talked in the world he'd grown up in. There'd been nothing but silences and hot accusations. His father had threatened, reviled, beaten. His mother had withdrawn into herself. There hadn't been room for him there.

There'd never been anyone to teach him how to communicate.

When Lucy felt his hands reaching for her, self-preservation kicked in. She batted them away. If he touched her, she'd fall apart completely.

"Leave me alone. You know how to do that. It's what you do best."

The accusation hit its mark, stinging, but there was nothing he could say to negate it. It was true.

"I did what I had to do."

"So do it again." It was a dare, a challenge. When he reached for her a second time, she began to pummel him with doubled-up fists. But he was stronger than she was and right now, more stubborn.

His arms closed around her. Lucy gave up the fight and collapsed, sobbing against his chest. Crying out her frustration, her fears, her relief that Alma hadn't been there to get in the way of whoever had broken into the shop.

She cried for Ritchie, for herself. And for what was and what would never be.

He held her to him and let her cry.

Chapter 9

Very carefully, Watley moved the tiny puzzle fragment he'd been studying from piece to piece on the folding card table, trying to match up the indentations and extensions. Beside him, on the floor, was the cover from the thousand-piece puzzle, showing him what it would ultimately look like. Three giant polar bears standing in the snow. He liked being challenged.

Part of the challenge was keeping his humor while trapped in an apartment with Dylan who was beginning to have more than a passing resemblance to a wounded bear.

Watley mopped his brow. "Want my advice?" he said.

Dylan didn't even spare his partner a glance, concentrating instead on their quarry across the street. The view through the camera lens brought the entrance right up to him. It was noon and the flow of customers was at a peak. "Not particularly."

"Well, I'm giving it to you, anyway." Watley frowned at the piece and for the moment, retired it as he picked up another one. "Free of charge. Don't ever move back east."

It was sticky in the apartment. The two floor fans did little to change that, moving the heavy air around only marginally. The weather had been particularly bad the last two days, with the humidity factor unusually high for Southern California.

But it wasn't just the weather that was getting to Dylan. It was the surveillance that appeared to be going nowhere despite the fact that they now had one of their men working inside the restaurant, taking the place that Ritchie had left vacant. It was the fact that he was getting nowhere in the investigation of the break-ins into Lucy's house and shop even though he knew in his gut who was responsible. And, it was the fact he'd spent the last ten nights sleeping on her sofa, hearing her and the baby just a few doors down. Picturing Lucy in his mind the way she looked as she was getting dressed and undressed. It was all of these things that were making him feel surly.

Most of all, it was the last thing that was really getting to him.

For lack of anything else to do, he adjusted the focus on the video camera. There were piles of videotapes against the wall, all neatly labeled and signifying nothing. "I'll cancel the movers."

With a triumphant smile, Watley pressed one puzzle piece into another, forming a union of white that looked very much like all the others he'd managed to connect together so far. "And while you're at it, I'd get ready to lose out on the Miss Congeniality award if I were you. It's not going to happen."

Dylan got up and crossed to the small refrigerator they'd brought in with them. Opening it, he took out a can of soda and popped the top. "Are you deliberately trying to start a fight?"

"Maybe." Watley raised his eyes from the puzzle and regarded his partner. "So I can find out what the hell has crawled under your skin and died there, making you so damned irritable."

Dylan took another long swig before trusting himself to give a civil answer. "Other than this investigation, which has taken almost four weeks to head exactly nowhere, and a partner who won't mind his own business?"

Watley picked up another piece. "Hey, in case you haven't realized it, you *are* my business. You're supposed to watch my back." He slanted a glance toward Dylan before looking down at the pieces again. "How are you going to do that if your head's someplace else?"

He didn't like being reminded of his responsibilities, even by someone he liked. "Don't worry about it, Watley. My head's just where it's supposed to be."

The look Watley gave him told Dylan his partner was unconvinced. "Can't tell by me."

Temporarily halting the recording, Dylan took out one tape and inserted a fresh one. "Can't tell a lot of things by you."

Watley had seen too many partnerships torpedoed by unavoidably close proximity. For all his distance, he liked McMorrow. The man was a solid cop, none better. For the sake of peace, he decided to change the subject. "Getting anywhere with Alvarez's sister?" Watley asked.

Dylan stopped labeling the tape. "What do you mean by that?"

The look in Dylan's eyes answered a lot of unasked questions for Watley. Dylan wasn't the only one who could piece things together. Smiling to himself, Watley moved another piece of the puzzle into place on the table. And another one in his head.

"I mean have you figured out yet what it was those jerks who broke into her place and her shop were looking for?"

Dylan blew out a breath and told himself he was getting too edgy. But the tightrope he was on was getting to him. He wasn't sure just how much longer he could maintain his balance.

Labeling it, he shoved the old tape back into its jacket and placed it on top of the pile. "Could be a microchip, could be a disk, a CD, although I'm leaning toward video. I don't know. But whatever it is," he told Watley grimly, "it's important enough to kill for."

"Don't you think it's about time you asked the captain for some police protection for the woman?" Watley said.

What did Watley think he'd been doing all this time? "She has police protection."

Watley waved his hand at Dylan. "Yeah, yeah, I know. Reed and Madigan and Saldana. And you. But all that's unofficial."

Dylan's shirt was sticking to his back and he longed to throw open a window. But they couldn't risk it. Any stray breeze would ruffle the curtains that were drawn to shield their camera.

It made it hard to keep his mind focused on the conversation. "I'd rather keep it that way. The whole thing is low-key. The less attention paid to her, the better."

Watley shrugged, going back to his puzzle. "If you say so."

Alma dug herself out of Lucy's overly comfortable chair. It was time to get going. She'd come over to drop off the inventory pages Lucy had requested and remained to coo over the baby and feel her heart melt to the consistency of a puddle within her chest. It was hard to believe that Dylan McMorrow had fathered such an adorable child. Not that the man wasn't good looking, she'd give him that. It was just difficult associating the word "adorable" with him.

"So how long is the Great Stone Man going to be staying with you?" she asked.

Eager to begin doing something productive, Lucy spread out the inventory sheets Alma had brought her all over the coffee table. Alma and Beth and Margaret had gone over the wreckage in the store and salvaged as much as they could. The items on the list that were too damaged to be sold as new were marked with only one-half of a cross instead of an *X*.

A cursory glance had told her that things weren't as bad as she had first thought. There was also nothing missing, not even a single video.

What was it they were looking for?

She realized that Alma was waiting for an answer. Too bad she didn't have one. "I don't know. Maybe until whoever tried to break in is caught."

Alma frowned. "Or until some whim makes him leave."

Lowering her eyes, Lucy began putting the sheets in order. "Drop it, Alma."

"No, you drop it." Her hand over the top form, Alma leaned forward until she got into Lucy's face, forcing her to look up. "You drop the brave act. This is me you're talking to, your best friend since pablum and strained beets. You can't lie to me."

With a determined movement, Lucy lifted Alma's hand and removed it from the sheets. "I'm not lying, Alma, I'm just trying to get this ready for the claims adjuster."

"The hell with the claims adjuster, how about the adjuster you're dealing with right now?"

That caught Lucy's attention. "What is it you're talking about?"

"I'm talking about the guy who 'adjusted' your life by upending it. Who 'adjusted' your heart, using it as a jump rope, then moving on. I'm talking about Elena's father, blind though he is." Alma shook her head, clearly mystified. "Any idiot with eyes could see that she's his daughter, why can't he?"

Lucy looked down at the sheets, but she'd lost the ability to concentrate. "You don't see what you don't look for."

"Great fortune cookie proverb," Alma snorted dismissively. She looked down at the baby, who was peacefully sleeping through all this in the bassinet she'd given Lucy as a baby shower gift.

"When are you going to tell him about her?" she asked more quietly.

"Never."

Alma looked at her in surprise. "Still?"

She couldn't believe that Lucy hadn't changed her mind, that she was still determined to keep Elena's parentage a secret from Dylan. It might have been different if Dylan had remained out of her life, but he was back and the opportunity was ripe.

"Look, much as there's no love lost between me and McMorrow, he *is* Elena's father. Don't you think he deserves to know that the two of you have gone forth to be fruitful and multiplied?"

Ordinarily, Alma would have made Lucy laugh. But not about this. "No."

"For heaven's sake, why?"

Giving up, Lucy let the sheets of paper drop back on the bright yellow tablecloth. "Because I don't want him that way."

"I thought you were so in love with him, you'd take McMorrow any way you could get him," Alma commented.

Yes, she had been in love with Dylan. Maybe still was, but she was ashamed of that. Ashamed that her pride had crumbled enough to let her contemplate that kind of a relationship. Because it would have been doomed from the very start.

"I've changed my mind. I don't want him that way. Because he felt an obligation to give Elena a full-time father." She felt her heart twisting inside her. "I don't want him out of a sense of duty. I want him because he loves me, and since that isn't going to happen, I definitely don't want him because he feels guilty.''

''Won't you feel guilty, not letting him know?'' Alma asked.

Lucy looked at the baby for a long moment. ''I'll deal with it.''

''If you want my advice, you've got enough to deal with without that.''

Lucy smiled warmly at her. ''I didn't ask your advise.''

Alma shook her head. ''What am I going to do with you?''

Lucy reached for Alma's hand and placed hers over it. ''Just be there for me.''

''You've already got that.''

Lucy's eyes crinkled, the way they had, Alma remembered, before any of this had started. The way they had when McMorrow had first entered her best friend's life. ''Then I don't need anything more,'' Lucy said.

Alma looked at her watch. ''Well, I'd better be getting back. Not that there's anything to be getting back for. Even if this break-in hadn't happened, we still wouldn't exactly be doing brisk business these days, what with the city tearing up every bit of available piece of sidewalk in front of the store in both directions.''

Lucy rose from the table, ready to accompany Alma to the door. ''Just keep telling yourself that this too shall pass.''

''Yeah.'' Alma laughed shortly. ''And when it does, something else equally as problematic will come and take its place.''

Same old Alma. Lucy slipped an arm around

her shoulders. "You're a born pessimist, Alma. Haven't I rubbed off on you at least a little after all these years?"

A grin played over Alma's lips. "Funny, I was just wondering the same thing about you." Stopping by the bassinet, she bent over and kissed the infant softly on the forehead. "Take care of her, Elena," she whispered to the baby. "She hasn't got enough sense to come in out of the rain."

Giving Alma a hug, Lucy stepped back. "I'll see you tomorrow," she reminded her.

Alma frowned. "You can call, fax or e-mail anything you've done. There's no reason for you to come in."

"I'll be the judge of that. Besides, there's still cleanup to do. I've been talking to Beth," she said when Alma raised a questioning eyebrow at her source of information. "I can't call, fax or e-mail that."

"What about Elena?" Alma asked.

"Elena will come with me, just like we planned." Lucy smiled fondly at the sleeping infant, her heart stirring. "About time she started pulling her own weight."

Alma allowed herself to be ushered to the door. "Right, high time. Slacking off this way for what, almost two weeks now?"

"Almost."

Alma could only shake her head as she left.

Dylan was getting accustomed to this, he realized as he pocketed the key Lucy had given him to the front door. He was accustomed to coming here at the end of the day instead of facing the solemn quiet of the apartment where he lived.

He turned the knob, entering. Behind him, Dylan heard Kane's vehicle driving away. He knew the danger in that, in getting too complacent. In expecting things and accepting them as part of his life. It set him up.

The warm aroma of food, tempting and spicy and about to be taken from the oven, greeted him before Lucy had a chance to call out to him.

"Hi. We're in the kitchen."

"Who's 'we'?" he asked, walking in.

He had his answer before she could say anything. Elena was sitting on the counter strapped into her infant seat, securely backed up against the wall.

"Why, Elena and me. Who were you expecting?" And then she looked at him. He looked as if he'd just walked home in the bottom of a pool. "Where did you spend the day, in a sauna?"

"Something like that."

She watched him as he stripped off his jacket, leaving it draped over the back of a chair. As careless as he was with his clothes, that was how careful he was with his weapon. Taking his holster and gun, he neatly wrapped the belt around it before placing it on top of the refrigerator next to the revolving spice rack she had.

"I'm not quite sure that exactly qualifies as a spice," she mused. He said nothing. She didn't really expect him to. "You're just in time."

She saw his eyes scan the room, as if he expected something to pop out. "For what?"

"Dinner, of course." The dining room felt too dreary tonight. She decided they'd eat in the kitchen. Removing the inventory sheets that had been spread out all over the surface, she'd set the table for two. "What did you think I meant?"

He shrugged, stopping to look at the baby. Elena made noises when he drew closer, as if she recognized him. He knew that wasn't possible. "Just wondered."

The heat had prompted her to become creative with a salad instead of making vegetables. She stopped lining up the ingredients and turned to look at him.

"I've had more scintillating conversations with my shoes. Is everything in your head classified, or can you divulge a few things now and then?"

He turned away from the baby. "I don't know what you're talking about."

Shredding the lettuce, she tossed it into a bowl and then began chopping tomatoes with more vigor than was necessary. "I'm talking about how you've become even more closemouthed than I remember you."

It was better to say nothing than to risk saying something he shouldn't. Something that might make her think that she was always on his mind.

"People change."

She stopped chopping, her eyes meeting his. "You don't. You stay constant."

Opening the refrigerator, he rummaged around for a bottle of beer. One was all he'd allow himself even if he was off duty. One wouldn't fog his brain. Finding it, he let the door close again. "So do you."

"Is that a compliment?"

He took the can opener and flipped open the cap. "If you want it to be."

She watched his Adam's apple move as he tilted the bottle back and took a long pull. Lucy fought an overwhelming urge to run her fingers along his throat. "What I want it to be is more."

He stopped drinking and looked at her. "More?"

"More." It wasn't that hard a word to understand. But maybe for him, it was. He was such a minimalist—except, she remembered, when it came to making love. Then the generosity of his spirit became very apparent. "More words, more meaning. More." Determined, she placed herself in his path as he turned away from the counter and her. "Talk to me, Dylan."

Why was she so set on getting under his skin? Didn't she know what she did to him? "I thought I was."

"No, I mean *really* talk. To *me*." She paused. When he said nothing, she tried again. "Okay, I'll help you out. I'll give you a topic. How's the investigation going?"

"Same as before."

She almost laughed then, not in abject defeat, but in amusement. The man could be so stubborn. But then, so could she. "I guess your mother never got a note from your teacher complaining that you were talking in class when you shouldn't be."

A hint of a smile played on his lips just before he took another long drink from the bottle. "Nope, she never did."

"If you think I'm going to give up on you—on getting you to hold up your end of a decent conversation," she amended when he raised a quizzical eyebrow at her, "you're wrong."

She could have sworn she saw amusement enter his eyes. "Knock yourself out."

Lucy had a feeling that she was going to have to. But there was no reason why, if they were forced together, they couldn't at least behave like two people who had shared a friendship if nothing more. Because, if they weren't friends in some context, then what was he doing here night after night, sleeping on a sofa that did nothing for his back?

"How long are you planning to sleep on the sofa?"

The question caught him off guard. He hadn't been expecting that one. "As long as it takes to keep you safe."

Tossing the tomatoes on top of the lettuce in the large salad bowl, she went on to select several zucchini. "Then your sleeping out there night after night might be counterproductive," she murmured more to herself than to him.

He didn't hear her. "What?"

Lucy shook her head, focusing on the zucchini she was slicing. "Never mind."

But she'd aroused his curiosity. He caught her hand by the wrist, stopping her and forcing her to look up at him. "What did you say?"

The smile on her face was enigmatic. "How does it feel to have the shoe on the other foot?"

"It pinches." Realizing that he was still holding her by the wrist, he released it, but he remained where he was. "What did you say?"

Free, she continued slicing. The rhythmic sound punctuated her words. "That maybe I'll never be completely safe. Does that mean you're planning on staying here indefinitely?''

There could be worse fates for him, he thought. But not for her. "Let's take it one day at a time."

The exact words she'd used in her mind when they had first begun their relationship. Odd that he should choose them. "Sounds promising."

He saw the look in her eyes and knew enough to be wary. "Lucy—"

Wriggling, Elena had decided to turn her whimper into a full-fledged cry, drawing both of their attention. Inspired, Lucy purposely continued chopping. "Uh-oh, sounds like someone needs to be changed." She looked at him innocently over her shoulder. "I've got my hands full, do you want to do the honors?"

"Honors?" he echoed.

She nodded her head toward the baby. "Change her."

Dylan stared at her incredulously. The first time he'd ever held a baby was during Elena's birth. He hadn't the slightest clue what to do with one after that. "Into what?"

"A clean diaper." Lucy bit back a laugh. It was the first time she'd ever seen Dylan at a complete loss. "You'll find them in my room. There's a changing table against the wall."

Dylan remained where he was. "I don't know a diaper pin from a bowling pin."

"The diaper pin closes. Besides, you're in luck. You won't need any kind of pin. I'm using the disposable kind."

Instead of picking up the infant, he elbowed Lucy aside at the table. "Why don't I take over what you're doing in the kitchen and you change Elena?'' It wasn't a suggestion, merely a statement of intent. He took the knife from her.

"Coward."

He wasn't about to argue with her. He knew where his strengths lay. "You've got that right."

"Put down the knife, tough guy, and come with me." Unstrapping Elena, she picked the infant up from the seat. "Dinner can wait."

"Look, I'm much better at this sort of thing."

But she shook her head. "Don't forget, I remember what your meals tasted like."

"This isn't a meal," he protested, "it's a salad."

"Which means that it's not about to go anywhere. You're a man, you're supposed to take pride in leaving yourself open to new experiences."

Where the hell did she pick that up? "I think helping you give birth should just about have that new experiences quota covered for the next six months."

She was a woman with a mission. Maybe she couldn't tell Dylan he was Elena's father, but since he was here, for however long he was here, she wanted him to take an active part in the little girl's life.

Very deliberately, Lucy hooked her free arm through his and began to usher Dylan out of the room. "Think again, tough guy."

Chapter 10

Dylan approached the changing table warily, standing just behind Lucy as she set the baby down. Saying he felt like a duck out of water didn't begin to cover it. More like an alien on someone else's home planet. Not fitting in never mattered to him one way or another. When it occurred, the fact barely registered.

But he knew when he was out of his depth and this certainly was it.

"Okay, she's all set for you." One hand still holding Elena in place, Lucy took a step back to give Dylan clear access to the baby.

Irritated at being put in this position, he maintained his ground and took refuge in his annoyance. "Look, there's no point to this."

Oh, no, he couldn't back out that easily. Now that she'd made up her mind, Lucy wasn't about to let him just waltz away. "There's a point to everything. You never know when this might come in handy.''

His dark eyebrows drew together for an even darker scowl. ''Police detectives don't get calls for emergency diaper changings.''

It amazed her how such a handsome face could turn so foreboding with just a simple shift of a few muscles. ''What if you came across an abandoned baby, crying and obviously uncomfortable because of an overloaded, soggy diaper? What then?''

Given the nature of his work, he doubted that was going to happen anytime soon. He conveniently ignored the fact that he hadn't thought he'd ever have to assist at a birth, either.

''I'd turn it over to my partner. Watley's expecting his first kid. Wears a beeper like some cross around his neck. By the time your little scenario comes around, he'd know what to do.''

The baby was kicking under her hand. Lucy continued looking at Dylan, unfazed by his attempt to shrug her off. ''What if you were alone?''

He blew out an exasperated breath. The woman had more staying power than tar. ''You don't give up, do you?''

Her eyes held his for a long moment. ''No, not always.''

Dylan knew what she meant, what wasn't being said. That she had given up on him as far as their relationship went. He also knew that it was all for the good, even if she didn't seem to think so.

So why did it feel as if someone was pulling his heart in two when he thought of spending the rest of his life without her?

Needing something to block the thought that had

sudden seemed bent on surrounding him, he surrendered to the likeliest candidate. Approaching the table, he looked down at the infant. How could anything so cute and innocent-looking smell so bad?

''Okay,'' he growled, ''let's get this over with.''

''Spoken like a trooper.'' Trying not to laugh at his pained expression, Lucy reached for a diaper and handed it to him.

Rome wasn't built in a day, she thought, but it looked as if it was finally going to be under construction.

Lifting Elena from the table, she patted the solidly padded behind as she smiled at Dylan. ''There, that wasn't so hard, was it?''

''Not the last time,'' he allowed.

Muttering something under his breath, he bent down to pick up the two previous diapers he'd attempted to put on. The ones that had fallen off because the tabs had lost their staying power after being applied and reapplied to the sides of the diaper as he'd attempted to make each in turn fit snugly. At this present rate of dexterity, every time Elena went to the bathroom it would cost five dollars to change her.

''Can't win the Kentucky Derby first time right out of the starting gate,'' she said glibly. ''But you never will if you don't try.''

Frowning, he dismissed her words as just so much meaningless noise. ''Don't see the connection.''

She wasn't about to explain it to him. That would be too much like preaching, and she had a feeling that nothing made Dylan shut down faster than a sermon. "Think about it." Elena safely tucked against her, she walked back into the kitchen. "Oh, by the way, I'm going back to work tomorrow."

He stopped in his tracks just past the doorway, staring at the back of her head. Was she crazy? It hadn't even been two weeks. "Why?"

Alma had said the same thing. She gave him the same answers. "Because there're a lot of things I can't do there from here. Because I'm going a little crazy just staying at home."

She wasn't one of those women who could become the perfect homebody, even if there hadn't been a living to earn. It just wasn't her style. She needed variety, somewhere to go so that coming home was special.

He pointed out the obvious. "You're supposed to be resting."

She readily dismissed that. "I've rested enough to carry me through the next ten years. I don't need much rest." Their eyes met as she raised them. And held for a long moment. "Remember?"

Yeah, he remembered. Remembered making love with her all night, feeling exhausted and invigorated at the same time. Remembered being amazed that her stamina surpassed his. Everything about Lucy always amazed him.

Things hadn't changed all that much, he thought now. Before he could think not to, Dylan touched her cheek, momentarily allowing himself a tiny respite from the ongoing vigil he was attempting to maintain over himself.

Lucy felt the pulse in her throat accelerate. It was hard for her to think when he was looking at her like that. She forced her mind onto other things. "Hungry?"

He didn't want to move, didn't want to drop his hand from her soft skin. But for his own survival, he did. "Not after seeing that dirty diaper."

"Let's see if we can fix that." Instead of placing Elena back in her infant seat, she handed the baby to him. "Here, you hold her, I'll finish the salad." She grinned at him. "Fair's fair."

Dylan doubted she really meant that. Fair would have been placing the baby into her seat and removing the infant from his line of vision. It wasn't fair to hand her to him, to make him hold her. To make him feel things.

He didn't want to feel things. Feelings only opened doors to places he had struggled to keep shut away. Places he had sealed years ago.

Places being with Lucy had managed to reopen again.

But he swallowed the very vocal protest that was hovering on his lips. Instead, he took Elena when Lucy thrust the infant into his arms. He took her and found himself looking down into wide blue eyes and a pouty little mouth that somehow managed, despite all his best efforts to the contrary, to bore a hole straight through his chest. Right into his heart.

He raised his eyes to look at Lucy's back. She was working quickly, competently, to complete the last component of their meal.

"I don't think you know the meaning of the word *fair.*"

Because her back was to him, he didn't see the smile widen on her lips.

* * *

"So, she talked you into letting her come in."

Alma's words of barely veiled disgust were meant for Dylan as he walked into the store behind Lucy, loaded down with the infant seat and a bag crammed full of necessary infant paraphernalia. Lucy had Elena in an infant sling snuggled warmly against her chest. Abandoning what she was doing, Alma crossed a length of floor that was almost completely cleared of debris to reach Lucy and the baby.

She cooed over Elena before glancing up at Dylan again. "Certainly shows what you're made of. I would have expected more of a show of strength from you. Serves me right for thinking highly of you, I guess."

The woman certainly didn't pull punches. "It's against regulations to tie up a new mother," he said tersely, unloading his burden on the first available surface he came to. "And there was no other way she was going to stay put." He looked at her darkly. "As her friend, you should know that."

His attention shifted to Lucy. He didn't like the idea of her being here, out in the open like this. Granted, the construction going outside tended to put people off and for the most part kept them from coming in, but that still left her rather accessible to the world at large.

Dylan stopped her as she began to slip the baby out of the baby sling. This was important and he wanted her full attention, even though he'd already told her this once. Odds were that she hadn't been listening.

"I've got a man outside. He's working as part of

the crew fixing the street. Anybody suspicious comes in, you call him.''

Alma laughed shortly. Glancing out the window, she couldn't tell one orange-draped man from another. ''And what's he going to do, pave the suspect?''

Dylan didn't even look in her direction. ''He's a cop, he'll know what to do.''

If Dylan wasn't going to kiss her, Lucy wished he'd stop finding reasons to get so physically close to her, she thought. It was ruining her ability to concentrate. And it certainly wreaked havoc on her determination to get over him.

''Moonlighting?'' she managed to ask.

As if suddenly realizing that he was still holding on to her, he dropped his hands from her shoulders, trying to block the impression of how small, how vulnerable she seemed.

''He owes me a favor.'' The explanation fell carelessly from his lips. He'd saved Gabe Saldana's life by pushing the other man out of the way and taking a bullet meant for him. It was part of the job as far as Dylan saw it. Saldana saw it differently.

There was probably a lot he wasn't saying, Lucy thought. She looked down at her daughter. She was being lulled by the sound of her parents' voices and her eyes were drifting shut. ''I guess so do I for all this protection.''

The less she felt she owed him, the better. Dylan avoided her eyes. ''You're feeding me regularly, so we're even.''

''Not by a long shot,'' she murmured.

A noise outside the shop had Elena starting. Fully awake, she seemed to stare at her surroundings. On a whim, Lucy held the infant up as if to allow her to get a better view of the store. "Someday, little one, all this'll be yours."

"Hey, don't scare the kid her first time here," Alma chided, drawing closer to Lucy. "Let her get used to responsibility gradually." She looked pointedly at her best friend, her voice dropping. "After all, remember who her father is."

Dylan stopped in the doorway. Though Alma's voice was low, he'd heard. Curiosity came first, but it didn't outdistance jealousy by much. Telling himself the emotion was childish and that he had no right to it did nothing to mute it. His eyes all but pinned Alma to the wall. "Who *is* Elena's father?"

Alma raised both her hands, palms up, warding off any further questions. "That's something you're going to have to get out of Lucy, not me." She took the baby from Lucy. "C'mon, kid, I've got a book in the back with your name on it." Grinning, she added, "Literally," before disappearing from the area.

For all intents and purposes, that left the two of them alone in the shop.

In terms of an investigation, Dylan wasn't one to let an opportunity slip by. He didn't now. Making his way to Lucy around a newly restored series of shelves, his eyes reached her first.

"Why won't you tell me who it is?"

Silently, she damned Alma for her glib tongue. "Because there's no point in your knowing."

He understood privacy. Lived by it. But they had been lovers. For a little while, they had been more. On some level, she owed him an explanation for finding another bed so quickly after he no longer shared hers.

"Why?" He struggled with the red-hot poker of jealousy that jabbed at his temper. "Are you afraid I might do something to him?"

She couldn't tell him, no matter how much she ached to. If she told him, then if he returned to her, she would never know what governed his actions—love or a sense of duty. Her back to the wall, she took the excuse he offered her.

"If that's what you think."

He'd never given her any reason to think of him as a violent man. He'd gone out of his way to be just the opposite because there was a monster inside of him he couldn't allow to become unleashed. "You know better than that."

Being near him only served to confuse her. "Me, I don't know much about anything." Restless, afraid of what she might admit, she looked at her watch. "Don't you have someplace else to be instead of here?"

He gave no indication that he heard her question. Instead, he studied her closely and realized something. "He still doesn't know, does he?"

Lucy pressed her lips together. He was hitting too close. She was torn between going deeper into the lie and admitting at least this much to him. What harm would it do if he knew that?

But she didn't have to make the admission, he read it in her face. "Why don't you get in contact with him and tell him?"

Galvanizing every fiber in her body, she forced herself not to waver. Not to look as if they were talking about him. "Because he isn't the kind of man I want as a father to my child."

Cynicism twisted his generous mouth. "A little late for that, isn't it?"

She deliberately turned his words into a personal attack. An attack was far easier to deal with. When attacked, you counter attack. You shore up your defenses. You didn't stand there, longing to fraternize with the enemy.

Her eyes narrowed. "Never too late to make amends. To try to fix something. His knowing wouldn't change things from what they were. He never wanted to be a father. It was just a short fling, that's all." At least, she assumed that's what it had been for him. For her it had been so very much more.

Which made her a fool, she couldn't help feeling.

Dylan felt as if something sharp and painful had just been flung in his face. "I thought you didn't believe in flings."

"So did I." And if she had stuck to her guns, she would have never allowed Dylan into her bed. Into her heart. Trying to seem blasé, she shrugged. "I lost my head." The opening notes of the "Sound of Music" disrupted the thick tension within the room, but Dylan ignored his cell phone. "Don't you think you should answer that? It's your life calling," Lucy said. He certainly didn't behave as if he had one outside the department, she thought.

Swallowing what would have been a sharp oath, Dylan angrily pulled out his cell phone and flipped it open. "McMorrow," he snapped.

"Damn, now I'm going to have to go for that

hearing test," Watley complained. "That's what I get for trying to do a good deed."

Dylan wasn't in the mood for games. "What the hell are you talking about?"

"I thought you might want to know some guy claiming to be your father is calling the station, asking for you. He talked to the desk sergeant." There was a pause on the other end of the line. "I thought you said your parents are dead."

"They are," Dylan told his partner without emotion.

"Huh. Well, this guy's alive and he claims he's your father. Says he wants to get in touch with you. Dispatch sent him through, thinking you were here. If you're interested, he left a number."

"I'm not interested," Dylan snapped. "Throw it away." There was no room for argument with the instruction. "I'm on my way in." He cut off the connection.

Turning, he started to leave but stopped when he felt Lucy's hand on his arm.

Maybe she didn't know him all that well, but she knew when something was really bothering him. "What was that all about? You turned as white as marble."

Instead of answering, Dylan glanced up at the recessed ceiling fixtures. "Looks like your lighting might need some work."

Why couldn't he answer anything directly? Was being honest with her such a hardship? She wasn't asking him to pledge his heart, she was asking him why the conversation he'd just had with the person on the other end of his cell phone had turned his face into a color rivaling freshly fallen snow.

Her hand on his arm tightened, holding him still a second longer. "Don't give me that. Whoever called just said something that got to you. Is it about Ritchie? About the break-ins?"

"No." Because he saw she didn't believe him and because he knew her imagination would run away with her if he offered her a nebulous lie to assuage her fears, he told her the truth. It didn't matter, anyway. "That was my partner. He said someone was calling in, claiming to be my father."

He'd never talked about his family with her, he'd just told her that his parents were both dead. She didn't understand what was going on. "Why would someone do something like that?"

He snapped before he caught the frayed end of his temper. "How the hell should I know?"

Lucy read between the lines. "*Was* it your father calling?"

He looked at her stonily. "My father's dead."

Without another word, he walked out of the shop. The bell above the door rang and shook as it slammed shut.

"Your father's not dead."

Dylan felt as if his nerves had been stretched tighter than a violin string across two frets. The monotony of surveillance had been counterbalanced by Watley's sporadic questions that thrust and parried into the fabric of the day. He was in no mood, coming to the store to pick up Lucy and her baby, to walk into the middle of an accusation.

One foot inside the door, he stared at her, surprise robbing him of what he knew was his limited ability for a quick comeback.

Crossing to him, trying to bottle up her own anger, Lucy closed the door behind him, shutting out the racket coming from jackhammers.

Ignoring her, he looked around the store. ''Where's Alma?''

''In the back.'' She wasn't about to let him divert her attention or worse, sweep her aside the way she knew he was trying to do. ''She has nothing to do with this and she won't save your hide.'' Moving quickly, Lucy presented herself squarely in front of him. ''Why did you lie to me? And don't bother denying it,'' she warned. ''You're not the only one with connections in this city. I had someone in Records at City Hall do a little digging for me. Your mother's dead, she died ten years ago, but your father's still alive. He works at SuperiorTech as a design engineer.''

He'd never seen her really angry before, not like this. The color in her cheeks was haunting. He shook himself free. ''You shouldn't have gone digging.''

She wouldn't let him shift blame onto her. It was his alone to bear. ''I have to when you won't tell me the truth about the simplest of things. Why would you lie to me about something like this?'' she demanded.

''I didn't.'' The simplest of things. If she only knew how complicated it all really was. That it was his father's fault that Dylan couldn't let himself live with her. Couldn't let himself love her. ''My father's dead to me.''

''Why?'' she asked when he said nothing further. ''What did he do?''

The planes on his face hardened. "That's none of your business."

Lucy felt her heart accelerating. She wasn't going to let him intimidate her. "I think it is. I think that whatever he did turned you into what you are today. An emotional hermit."

He wasn't going to debate this with her. He wasn't good with words the way she was. But for him, silence worked just as effectively.

"Think whatever you want. I can't stop you." Determined to do what he had come to do, Dylan crossed to Elena and picked the baby up from her infant seat. Without looking at Lucy, he asked, "You ready to go home?"

She sighed, picking up her things. "Yes. I just wish you were."

"You've been around greeting cards too long," he told her tersely. "You're beginning to sound like one, sentimental and syrupy."

Lucy made the best of it. At least he was still talking. And if he talked, maybe she could get something out of him.

"Nothing wrong with that," she countered. "A little old-fashioned sentiment and syrup is good for you."

"Only if you're a pancake." He was already at the door, scooping up the infant seat in his other hand, leaving Lucy to carry the bag.

She drew the strap over her shoulder, setting her purse strap on top of that. Raising her voice, she called out, "I'm leaving, Alma."

"Good." Alma's disembodied voice came from the back office. "I'll come out when the smoke clears."

Dylan's frown deepened as he held the door open for her with his back. "You'd better tell that woman to stop listening at keyholes."

"Keyholes?" Lucy hooted. "When you raise your voice the way you just did, people in Maine look over their shoulders."

Scanning the street scene, he exchanged looks with an undercover policeman before continuing on to where he had parked his car. He indicated the baby with his eyes. "Doesn't seem to scare her any."

Pride had Lucy's face softening with a fond smile. She was absolutely, completely in love with her baby. "She's gutsy."

"Like her father?"

He didn't miss an opportunity, did he? "Maybe," she conceded lightly, then smiled smugly. "But definitely like her mother."

There was no way Dylan could argue with that. In his opinion, Lucy could hold her own with anyone. It was one of the things that had drawn him to her in the first place. The strength he felt radiating from her. Strength and optimism with just a small dash of vulnerability thrown into the mix.

If he were being honest with himself, he had to admit that had hooked him as well, though he'd always done his best to steer clear of vulnerable women. Women who reminded him of his mother.

But Lucy's vulnerability had just drawn out the protective side of him. That had been his first clue that he was in over his head and in trouble. Because she managed to ensnare him with every aspect of her. And being tightly wrapped around a woman would only make him that much more susceptible to the demons he knew were in his blood. Demons he'd inherited from his father. Demons that would make him eventually hurt her.

Dylan would have rather cut off both his arms than to ever hurt Lucy. So he'd done the next best thing. He'd left.

She groaned as she got into the car. His reflexes snapping into place, Dylan had his hand on his holster as he looked around, ready for anything. But there was nothing out of the ordinary in the scene he saw.

"What's the matter?"

She fastened her seat belt, mentally upbraiding herself. "I forgot to take the pork chops out of the freezer to defrost them and the microwave is on the blink. That leaves us with a choice of a late dinner, or Popsicles."

"No problem." Dylan slid in behind the steering wheel. Would that everything else were this easy to remedy. He turned, making sure the infant seat was secured one last time. "I figured you'd be too tired to cook." He turned on the ignition, then pulled away from the curb. "There's Chinese takeout in the trunk. If we don't hit traffic, we can have it while it's still warm." He saw the smile curving her mouth as he got in. "What?"

That explains the tempting aroma within the car that was beginning to register, Lucy thought. "Just when I give up on you, you do something sweet."

He shrugged. "I've got to eat, too."

Leaning forward just as they came to a red light, she pressed her fingertips to his lips. "Don't spoil it. Let me savor the moment."

He curbed the sudden, strong urge to kiss her

fingers. Instead, he removed her hand and muttered, "Buckle up."

Her eyes danced as she sat back. "I already have—and the ride's not as bumpy as you think."

Dylan felt silence was his best option.

Chapter 11

Slipping the key into his pocket, Dylan walked in quickly, trying not to think how strange it felt to be in Lucy's house and not hear sounds that were already becoming so familiar to him. In a little more than two weeks' time, the routine he followed had become more a part of him than anything he'd done all the years that had come before.

Coming home to her and then, for the last few days, with her at the end of a long day somehow seemed far more right to him than walking into his own empty apartment ever had.

He found himself listening for the sound of her voice, or the baby's whimper, even though he knew they weren't here. Lucy and Elena were both at her shop. He'd purposely picked this time to do what he had to do without distractions.

For the last few days, he'd come here just a little after two, when the flow of patrons entering and leaving the Den of Thieves was at a low ebb, to slowly, methodically sift through the things in Lucy's house. Looking for what had been overlooked by both the police and the men who had broken in.

So far, he'd found nothing that remotely looked as if it would have been worth the sacrifice of a life.

Though he'd been the one to put things away after the break-in, it had been done quickly. Then he'd wanted to get things ready for her return. He hadn't the time to sift and search.

Common sense told him he probably wouldn't find anything now, but common sense had been known to be wrong.

Walking into Lucy's bedroom, he forced himself to shut out the memories and proceed with what he had to do. He was, first and last, a police detective. If there was something small left in the middle, he wasn't about to pay any attention to it. It would only interfere.

But he found himself standing before her bed. Though she'd gotten up late, she'd still taken the time to make it before she left. He would have expected nothing less. Lucy liked to have all the details of her life neat and well organized. Something you would have never guessed just by looking at her. The first time he'd seen her, she'd seemed like such a free spirit. Lightning in a bottle, about to blow out the cork.

Rousing himself, he crossed to her walk-in closet and opened it. That, too, was organized. No haphazard toss of a blouse here, a skirt there. Everything was hung up, facing the same direction, coordinated by color. Husbanded the way someone who had grown up with nothing, appreciating every tiny new thing, would have done.

He brushed against the sleeve of a blue silk blouse as he reached for the box that was overhead on the shelf. For a second, he paused and allowed himself one small indulgence, here, in the recesses of her closet, where no one could see. He raised the sleeve to his cheek and let the soft fabric glide along his skin. Dylan felt his stomach tightening as the faint scent of her perfume drifted into his consciousness.

Damn, he couldn't stand here, mooning like some pathetic, lovesick adolescent. He had a job to do. There had to be some shred of something he could find to tie some of the ends together, bring at least this part of the investigation to a close and get him to move out of her life.

Dylan dropped the sleeve in self-disgust and reached for the box. Taking it down, his fingers came in contact with what felt like an envelope.

Curious, he stretched and reached in farther. It was an envelope. Business-size and manila, its flap was worn as if it'd been the victim of numerous openings and closings.

Forgetting the box which he'd already gone through once when he'd cleaned away the debris, Dylan sat down on her bed and opened the envelope.

There were photographs inside. A handful of what appeared to be candid shots. Of memories chemically sealed in time. He stared at the photograph on top. It was of him. Looking at the background, he tried to remember when it could have been taken. He didn't recall posing for it. But then, Lucy liked to wield that small camera of hers like a professional. Gobbling up moments in time so that she could look at them later, she said. He never liked having his picture taken. It hadn't stopped her.

His mouth curved in a smile that was both fond and grim as he slowly went through the photographs. Some of the backgrounds were familiar, some nudged only vague recollections.

He paused, looking at a photograph that was different from the others. This one was of the two of them. He was standing behind her, his arms encircling her, and he looked as if he was saying something in her ear. She was laughing. There was a kiddie ride just behind them. This was taken at the annual fair Bedford held, he remembered. Ritchie had been with them. She must have given the camera to him and told him to take the shot. Ritchie wasn't the kind to do something like this on his own. He hadn't been interested in memories, only the present—and the future.

Neither of which he had any longer, Dylan thought grimly.

With the tips of his fingers, he slowly outlined Lucy's face, so close to his. He remembered that day. Remembered the sound of her laughter, running in his ears. Filtering down to his soul. That was when he'd still thought that...

Dylan frowned, it didn't matter what he thought. That he'd believed maybe he wasn't like his abusive father. That he could break the chain. He'd discovered shortly thereafter that he couldn't. The rage, the jealousy that had overtaken him when he thought Lucy was seeing someone behind his back showed him otherwise. It had taken everything he had to shut the lid down on it. When he'd discovered it was all a mistake, that she'd been meeting with the man, the husband of a friend of hers, to plan a surprise party for the woman, it had all come crashing in on him. The relief that she had been faithful was outweighed by the reinforcement of his beliefs that he could never marry Lucy. Never be the kind of husband she deserved. The specter of his father, hiding in the shadows, was only waiting to emerge. He couldn't risk it. Or Lucy.

Dylan tossed the photograph aside, searching through the remaining stack. Why was she keeping these photographs while she had none of Elena's father? He'd already been through the albums she kept, all neatly organized and arranged according to date order. He hadn't expected to find any photographs of himself there, and he hadn't only because she'd kept them separated. So why weren't there any of Elena's father somewhere?

It didn't make sense to him.

Very carefully, he slipped the photographs back into the envelope, and then returned it to its place. He didn't want Lucy to know he was going through her things, he knew she'd balk at it. Strictly speaking, it was an unlawful search. He was bending the rules, but it was necessary.

What it wasn't, he was beginning to think, was fruitful. With a sigh, he finished looking through the box of keepsakes and returned it to its place as well.

Dylan was beginning to entertain the idea that maybe there wasn't anything to find. Maybe Ritchie had just been talking, blowing hot air. It wouldn't have been the first time.

But this time, it apparently had cost Ritchie his life.

Still, Dylan felt he had to proceed as if it were true, as if there was something tangible to go on. Which meant having to deal with a great many old memories he'd shut away.

Memories that came leaping out at him at the worst possible times.

Quickly, he finished checking the pockets of her skirts and carefully moved the hangers back into position. Nothing in her pockets, nothing inside any of the shoes that were so neatly lined up on the floor. In the back of his mind, he knew he was searching for some sort of videotape, but even that wasn't certain. There might be something else to go on, something else to lead him where he wanted to go. Out of habit, he glanced at his watch as he shut the closet.

If he didn't get back soon, he figured he'd probably find his partner swinging off a light fixture. Between the monotony of waiting for something to happen outside the restaurant, waiting for his wife to page him, and staring at indistinguishable white puzzle pieces that were still spread out all over that damned folding card table of his, Watley struck him as a man who looked as if he was coming to the end of his rope.

Dylan nodded at the off-duty detective sitting in the unmarked car across the street as he hurried to his own vehicle. He wasn't sure just how much longer he was going to be able to pull in favors and have men guarding Lucy's house like this. Especially when there was nothing to show for it.

"Aren't your friends getting a little tired of playing musical detective yet?" In reply to the silently raised eyebrow, Lucy nodded at the unmarked car they passed as they pulled out of her driveway the following morning. She recognized the man as Kane Madigan. "It's been more than two weeks now and I'd think that they'd want to get on with their lives." Shifting in her seat, she looked at Dylan. "For that matter, I'd think you'd want to get on with yours as well."

"This is my life."

He wasn't talking about her, but the job. She knew enough not to take the comment personally. She'd made that mistake before about Dylan, taking ambiguous words and making them personal. Thinking that they had something special when he was only passing through.

She tried to sound nonchalant. "Guarding supposed victims?"

Dylan heard the edge that came into her voice and ignored it. He didn't feel like getting into anything. "Yeah."

She glanced behind her to make sure that Elena wasn't uncomfortable. A shiny, toothless face looked back at her. Did he see it, she wondered, the resemblance between himself and the baby? Did it register subconsciously?

"I'm beginning to think there was no connection between the two break-ins, other than just a very bad streak of luck." She turned forward again. "Nothing else has happened."

She hadn't told him about Palmero calling. Twice since the funeral, each time suggesting that they get together. She felt like a fly saying no to a spider's invitation. Although she certainly thought he was slimy and untrustworthy, she couldn't make herself believe the man had her brother killed. And she was afraid that if she told Dylan the man had made advances, Dylan might fly off the handle at him. She'd decided that Palmero was just hoping to prey on what he perceived to be her vulnerable state. She'd known men like that before.

"Are you trying to get me off your sofa?" Dylan asked.

She'd always been strong when she had to be. Why did her grasp on that strength waver so badly whenever it came to him? "I'm trying to get us both to move on with our lives."

Taking a turn slowly, he guided his vehicle onto a major thoroughfare. At this hour of the morning, the last of the rush hour traffic was finally beginning to dissipate. "I'll move on, Lucy, when I'm sure you're safe."

She wanted him gone, yet the thought of not seeing him, of knowing that each day would go by without him in it, dragged tiny, sharp nails across her heart. She had to stop this waffling, she upbraided herself. "And when will that be?"

"When we get whoever killed Ritchie."

The grim answer reminded her that there were far larger issues involved here than just her heart. "You still think whoever did it is the one who broke into my house and my store?"

He noticed she didn't mention Palmero by name and wondered if she'd decided that the man hadn't a hand in it after all. Dylan lifted a shoulder and let it drop carelessly. "Seems logical to me."

She stared at his profile for a long moment. Damn it, why, after everything that she'd been through, everything she knew about him, was she still in love with this man?

Love and *lunacy* began with the same letter, she reminded herself.

"And you think you might find him by going through my things?" The look of surprise on his face pleased her. He'd obviously thought she wouldn't catch on.

"How did you…?"

The photographs had been out of order. She'd taken them down last night, prompted by a strong yearning to return to a time when she had still believed in happy endings and that life could be as tidy as her shop. His photograph had always been on top. This time, she discovered the one that had been taken of the two of them at the fair was in its place.

Lucy smiled at him like someone with a secret that she intended to hold on to just a little longer. "You're not as good as you think you are about putting things back. What are you hoping to find?"

Not what he had found, Dylan thought, easing into the flow of traffic on MacArthur Boulevard. "Whatever it is that whoever broke in missed. Something that's maybe out in plain sight."

Traffic came to a dead stop. There were orange cones equidistantly distributed in the next lane, slowly eating up the space and inching their way over to the next lane. Three lanes were reduced to one while someone in their infinite wisdom mandated that the road to the medical complex they were heading toward was under construction.

Queuing up behind the electric-blue sports car, Dylan spared her a grim look. "Something Ritchie would have died for."

She gave voice to what had been bothering her from the very first. "I don't understand that. Why wouldn't Ritchie have told them what they wanted to know? Why die for it?"

Dylan had had trouble with that himself at first. "Revenge. Ritchie was smart enough to know that once they had him in that situation, they'd kill him one way or another. He didn't want to give them the satisfaction of handing over what they desperately wanted."

It still didn't make any sense to her. "Which would be?"

"Some kind of evidence. Something to blackmail them with. If we knew what, then I'd know what I was looking for."

The next lane finally began to open up. Glancing behind him, he took his opportunity and got into the lane. Without any other cars in front of him, he made up for lost time. They had appointments to keep, or at least, she did.

"Why don't you have any photographs of him?"

The question caught her off guard. It took her a second to answer. "I've got plenty of photographs of Ritchie."

"No, I mean him." She knew who he was talking about, he thought. He realized that his hands had tightened on the steering wheel and he forced himself to slacken his fingers. Dylan nodded back toward the baby strapped into her seat. "Elena's father."

Familiar wavering began within her. Lucy refused to pay attention to it. Instead, she kept her face forward, looking through the windshield. "It didn't last long enough for me to take a photograph."

"It lasted less than ten seconds?"

She ignored the biting sarcasm in his voice. "Felt like it."

Guilt pressed heavily down on him. "Was that my fault?"

Unable to help herself, she slanted a look at him. "Are you asking defensively, or curiously?"

Frustrated, annoyed, wishing he could just drop the matter and concentrate on what they were paying him to do, he grated, "Whatever way will get me an answer."

He wouldn't even give her that much, would he? Wouldn't even let her know if he was jealous or if it didn't matter.

She drew herself up like a queen, invisible shields going up around her. "Then my answer is don't waste time going over something in the past. What's done is done. The only way you live is to move on." She struggled with the tears she felt forming, forbidding herself to cry. Her voice was quiet when she spoke again. "I learned that a long time ago."

Dylan had sworn to himself that he wouldn't pry, wouldn't push, but the question had been eating away at him ever since he'd seen her rounded belly filled out with someone else's child. "Why won't you tell me who it is?"

She resisted the temptation to wrap her arms around herself for comfort. Dylan was far more in tune to body language than he was to feelings. "Because I don't want you to know."

It didn't take a brain surgeon to figure that part out. But why? he wondered. "Is it someone I know?"

Her smile, when she offered it, was sad. "It's not even someone I know."

"Damn it, Lucy—"

Her head snapped up as she suddenly recognized her surroundings.

"We're here." Dylan pulled into the first available medical complex parking spot. She'd already unbuckled her seat belt and was gathering her purse to her. "If you drop us off, we can get a cab back. Or call Alma—"

Damn it, she looked like a woman eager to jump ship. Why wouldn't she answer him? "I'm not dropping you off." Getting out, Dylan quickly rounded the hood, moving fast to block her way before Lucy had a chance to lift Elena out, infant seat and all, and make her getaway.

Lucy stared at him. She hadn't expected this. "You're coming in with me?"

Taking Elena from her, he led the way into the brightly lit, eight-story building, one of five that made up the complex. "Looks that way."

Lucy found herself hurrying to keep up with him. Just when she thought she saw a pattern, he did something unpredictable and messed everything up. At this rate, she was never going to understand him.

Not that, she figured, she'd have much time to

puzzle him out firsthand. He'd be gone again soon, the only thing that was uncertain was when.

"Why, do you think the doctor's going to hold us hostage...?" she quipped dryly.

He stopped at the bank of elevators, pressing the button for the next available car, ignoring the fact that the three other people who were waiting had already pressed the button ahead of him. "I hope Elena's not going to pick up on that sarcasm of yours."

The car arrived and she followed him in. Lucy pressed the button for the second floor. "Why not? Best defense she could get."

As they stepped off the elevator, he opened his mouth, then shut it. He then gave in to the impulse that had been tugging so madly at him for so long that he'd lost all track of time. Holding the infant seat and its occupant against him with one hand, he snagged Lucy with his free hand and pulled her to him.

Her gasp of surprise ended against his mouth as he kissed her—hard—right there in front of the bank of elevators on the second floor, with people getting off another car, hurrying to keep their appointments.

Lucy went from zero to intoxicated in a second. Her head spun and her blood surged through her. She fought the urge to give herself up to the sensations slamming through her like race cars coming out of a tailspin and careening into brick walls. This wasn't the time or the place.

But if she thought that, why didn't he? He was the last word in private, always had been, and what he was doing right now was the complete antithesis of private.

Not at all certain if her knees hadn't permanently locked in place to keep her from sliding onto the floor, she drew back. It took her a second to focus on him. ''What was that?''

''The best defense against your mouth I can mount.''

She was having trouble dragging air back into her lungs. Still shaky, she pressed her fingers to her mouth before trying to speak again. ''You really think so?''

Because another car had stopped and there were people beginning to disembark, he motioned her toward the corridor and the doctor they were going to see. ''Got you to stop talking for a minute, didn't it?''

She couldn't argue with that.

Dr. Rafe Saldana was running behind schedule thanks to a faulty alarm clock and a night of hospital rounds that had ended in the wee hours of the morning. He didn't like shortchanging his patients by hurrying them along. This meant he was going to have to cancel lunch with his wife and work straight through. He hoped Dana wouldn't be too disappointed. He knew he was. Picking up the chart that had been posted outside the door, Rafe promised himself to make it up to her.

Right now, he had a new patient to see to. Nodding, he smiled at them. The husband, he noted, was scrutinizing him as if he was intent on performing a dissection right then and there. It wasn't uncommon in a first time father and Rafe didn't take it personally.

The pair, he thought looking at the baby who was stripped down to her diaper, did nice work. But then, they were a fine looking couple.

Rafe put out his hand to the man. "Mr. Alvarez, hello, I'm Dr. Saldana. I met your wife in the hospital right after I examined Elena." Sheila Pollack had come to him, the way she always did when the new mother didn't have a pediatrician already picked out, and asked that he examine the newborn. He had a very soft spot in his heart for Sheila. She'd been the one to refer Dana to him. "You have a beautiful daughter."

Hearing the pediatrician refer to Elena as Dylan's daughter, Lucy felt her heart tighten within her breast. It took her a moment before she could collect herself enough to correct the doctor.

"Oh, no, he's not Mr. Alvarez—"

"Elena's not mine," Dylan told him tersely. It suddenly occurred to him that he almost mourned that declaration. He hadn't realized, until this moment, that part of him actually wished that she was his daughter. "I'm just a friend."

The label, so stilted, so lifeless, felt heavy on his tongue. Worse, it felt like a lie. He wasn't a friend. He was a man in limbo, stuck between heaven and hell and not knowing which was which or what direction to turn. As an afterthought, he gave the doctor his name. "Dylan McMorrow."

"My brother has mentioned a Dylan Mc-Morrow," the doctor replied.

Saldana. The connection suddenly penetrated. "Is your brother Gabe Saldana?"

"Right." Rafe clasped Dylan's hand again, shaking it firmly. "He told me you saved his life."

Dylan didn't have an opportunity to downplay the incident. Lucy had made a sudden connection of her own. "You're related to the man sitting outside my house in the wee hours of the morning?"

Gabe didn't talk about his work with any frequency, but this had been unofficial and off the record. And the reason he and Dana hadn't been able to get together with Gabe and his wife in the last two weeks. Rafe looked at the mother of his patient with new understanding.

"You're the woman he's guarding?" Rafe laughed shortly, shaking his head. "Well, well, well, small world."

And it was getting smaller all the time, Lucy thought, glancing at Dylan.

Sheila Pollack pushed back on the stool she was sitting on, pulled off her plastic gloves and deposited them into the wastepaper basket with precision. She smiled reassuringly at her patient.

"You can get dressed now, Lucy." Sheila picked up the chart and made a notation. "I must say, you've made one of the fastest recoveries I've ever seen." She glanced back several pages to double-check the figures. "Amazing. You're down to the weight you were before you became pregnant and your body's completely back in sync." She let the pages fall back into place and closed the chart. "Someone must be taking very good care of you."

Already off the table, Lucy was hurrying into her clothes. The sooner she got ready, the sooner Dylan could drop her and Elena off at the shop and get back to his own work. He'd lost enough time because of them as it was.

She stepped into her skirt and pulled it up. "In a manner of speaking."

Holding the chart to her, Sheila paused. "I caught a glimpse of him outside in the waiting room with Elena. Same man who brought you in, right? The police detective. Dylan McMorrow, wasn't it?"

"Right, Dylan McMorrow." Lucy avoided her doctor's eyes. "He's just a friend."

"I see." He was more than that, Sheila thought. Anyone with eyes could see that there was something going on between the two. It didn't take inherent intuitiveness to spot that. "It's none of my business, Lucy, but if you need someone just to talk to, you've got my home phone number."

Sheila had given it to her when Lucy had first discovered she was pregnant and alone, for all intents and purposes. "I appreciate it, but there's nothing to talk about. Really."

Sheila placed a hand on her shoulder, the simple gesture speaking volumes. "Okay. For now, just take comfort in knowing that all systems are go." Sheila caught her eye. "All systems," she emphasized.

Finished dressing, Lucy picked up her purse as she slipped on her shoes. She strove for levity. "Meaning I can return to my career as a fighter pilot?"

"That, and even stop to get romantically involved with another fighter pilot if the occasion arises."

Despite the unexpected kiss, Lucy sincerely

doubted that Dylan wanted to do anything other than just his job when it came to her. "No chance of that," Lucy said.

She'd heard that before, Sheila thought. And even believed it true when it came to her and Slade—before he'd become her husband. She was living proof that nothing was ever written in stone. "Where there is life, there's hope, and chance finds us in very strange places in our lives," Sheila said to Lucy. Their eyes met and she smiled. "For the record, I think he's very good-looking in a dark, brooding way."

"Dark and brooding." Lucy rolled the phrase over on her tongue. "That about sums him up."

Lucy first saw his reflection in the row of frames she had on display against the back wall. Dylan was walking toward her. With flowers. Spinning around, she saw that it wasn't a trick of light, he had a mixed bouquet of daisies and carnations clutched in his hand, their heads bowed toward the floor and bobbing as he strode toward her.

"What's the occasion?"

"No occasion."

He thrust them toward her like a peace offering, except that there had been no declaration of war, no recent battles to recover from. Only the one that had originally been fought when he had walked out on her. He shrugged, looking around for Elena.

"There was a kid selling flowers at the freeway exit. He looked down on his luck." Selling flowers at freeway exits had been the way Dylan had first tried to earn some money—so that he could take his mother away someplace where she could be safe from his father. "I thought I'd help him out. You can put them in water or throw them away, makes no difference to me."

Oh, no, he wasn't going to pull that again. She saw through him. "Yes, it does. Why do you say things like that?" She looked at the bouquet. A couple of the flowers were wilting, but it only seemed to enhance his gesture. "If I tossed these out, some part of you would be hurt."

He was beginning to regret his rash action. He should have known she'd make too big a deal out of this. "You give me too much credit." Seeing the baby in her seat, he made his way over to her.

Lucy followed him, determined to get him to admit to having some sort of feelings. Actions might speak louder than words, but she wanted at least one of the words, too. "No, you don't give yourself enough credit."

Unable to help himself, he grinned at Elena. "You don't know what you're talking about. I know I'm a good cop."

Doggedly, Lucy got in his face. "But you don't seem to know you're a good man, too. You went out of your way with Ritchie, with that boy selling flowers." She gestured toward her daughter. "I've seen you with Elena when you don't think I'm around. There's a soft, sweet side to you, Dylan McMorrow, no matter how much you try to deny it. I've seen it, so you can't lie to me," she insisted.

Their eyes met and held for a long moment. And then he shrugged. "Maybe you should go back to your doctor. You're obviously delusional."

"I can see clearly, Dylan. And what I see—"

He didn't want to hear what it was she thought

she saw. He had already ventured too far on a path he wasn't supposed to be taking. "Maybe you're right. Maybe you don't need me sitting guard on this sofa night after night. Maybe—"

She blocked the hurt his words evoked. "What are you afraid of, Dylan?"

He wanted to saying "nothing," but it was a lie. And lies died when the truth was stronger. "You."

The quiet admission took her by surprise. Anticipation surged through her. She took a breath. "My mother used to say you should never run from your fears, but face them. Head to head. Toe to toe."

His eyes washed over her face, lingering on her mouth. "Did she say anything about lip to lip?"

A smile curved hers. "She forgot that part."

But he hadn't.

Dylan took her into his arms and kissed her.

Chapter 12

He lasted another week.

Dylan hadn't thought it possible, but somehow he had managed to make it through an entire week. Seven more days of keeping everything within him self-contained and bottled up.

But he knew himself and knew it was just a matter of time before the bottle shattered and what was inside it would come spilling out, drenching not only him, but Lucy as well. It was her he was thinking of now.

Her he was always thinking of.

Her voice, her laughter, her face, the light fragrance she wore that clung to her clothing and to the very air she passed through. And to him even when he tried to keep his distance.

Standing now in her living room, with dusk softly creeping in to prepare the way for night, Dylan stared at the sofa with the bedding she'd put out for him and contemplated words he'd said to her a week ago in her shop.

Maybe he shouldn't be here any longer.

They had driven home from the shop that evening in relative silence, emotions riding with them like silent, uninvited third parties. Alma had walked in on them earlier and interrupted the kiss that hovered between them, making it evaporate. Even after she'd realized her mistake and gone back into the storeroom, bidding them good-night, Dylan had abruptly retreated back into his armor. Back behind the barricades that had been erected to keep everyone out and himself in.

It was safer that way.

But it wasn't more comfortable. Not anymore. Maybe it never had been, but it had been what he'd known and there was a certain comfort in that, in the familiar.

Dylan fingered the edge of the pillowcase now, debating his next move. If he were being honest with himself, he hadn't been comfortable inside his own skin for a very long time. The life he'd chosen, the one he'd fashioned for himself, no longer satisfied the marginal requirements he had.

Nothing felt right anymore.

The niche he'd attempted to reclaim after he'd walked away from her that first time, almost ten months ago, no longer fit. Nothing fit. Wanting Lucy had done that to him.

Dylan let the pillow drop back on the sofa. It slipped, falling to the rug unnoticed. He couldn't remain here, feeling this way. Knowing that if he released his hold on his feelings even just a little, a myriad of emotions would spring out all over the place like so many jack-in-the-boxes, simultaneously set off.

Edgy, wanting to tell her of his decision before he weakened and changed his mind again, Dylan looked toward the doorway leading into the hall, willing her to walk in.

She didn't.

He knew where she was. In the baby's room, getting Elena ready for bed. He'd woken up early Sunday morning to find her there, working to transform Ritchie's room into a nursery. There'd been tearstains on her face, the only evidence of her feelings as she packed away the last of her brother's things. Not knowing what to say, he pretended not to notice.

Instead, he gruffly volunteered his services when he saw her tackling the job of putting the crib together. He'd been just in time to rescue her from being done in by the springs when they came loose and almost fell on her. She'd been on her stomach at the time, screwing two sections of the railing together. She remained the most stubborn woman he knew.

When they'd finished, she'd said something about his being good with his hands. Though he shrugged it off, the compliment had warmed him. In the privacy of his own mind, he'd had to admit that there'd been a certain amount of satisfaction, standing back and looking at the crib, knowing he'd been the one to put it together.

He'd derived a great deal of satisfaction these last few weeks, helping Lucy care for Elena, more than he would have expected. More than he was accustomed to. Even solving a crime hadn't felt like this, and up until three weeks ago, he would have sworn that was all he was about. Just his job. He was convinced that he had been completely hollowed out by his years of watching his parents interact; his job was all he had ever intended to be about.

But now he wasn't sure anymore.

He wasn't sure about anything. Except that loving Lucy would be a mistake.

With a sigh, he made his way to the baby's room.

The door was ajar, with traces of light seeping out along the edges. The low sound he heard crept to him like the dusk. Slowly. Soothingly.

She was singing to Elena, he realized. Humming was more like it. The sound went completely through him, embedding itself in his bones.

The tips of his fingers on the door, Dylan pushed it open, not wanting to startle her and risk waking the baby. Her face averted from the door, Lucy was sitting on the rocking chair, the one she'd fallen in love with when they'd gone to the flea market more than ten months ago. She'd dragged him there and he'd pretended it was against his will, but he'd secretly enjoyed seeing the way her face lit up when she came across what she called a "treasure" that someone else in their short-sightedness had thrown away.

The rocking chair had seemed like a hapless piece of junk to him, but because she wanted it, he'd bought it for her, telling her she had a weakness for things that looked as if they were beyond hope. She'd only smiled at him then, and told him to wait and see.

He'd left her less than two weeks later.

The rocking chair was fully restored now. She'd

reinforced the broken arm, stripped off the coats of
varnish, sanded it and then lovingly applied coat
after coat of stain before sealing it all with a wa-
terproof coat.

The rocking chair was a symbol, he thought, a
symbol of how stubborn she could be when she set
her mind to something and what her determination
could accomplish.

He thought of Elena's father. The man was a
jackass to have walked out on Lucy.

It took Dylan a moment to realize that Lucy
wasn't just singing the baby to sleep, she was nursing her. Mesmerized, he stood and watched her.
The scene seemed so natural, so beautiful in its innocence, he debated slipping away before she noticed him.

But he couldn't get himself to move. Instead, he
remained where he was in the doorway, watching.
Wishing with all his heart that he could claim to be
part of this instead of just someone on the outside,
looking in. But his conscience wouldn't allow him
that luxury.

When Lucy raised her eyes to his, looking so
seductive and beatific at the same time, he thought
he was going to swallow his tongue. Lucy placed
her finger to her lips, then indicated Elena with her
eyes. The baby had fallen asleep.

Holding his breath, he watched her as she slowly
rose to her feet, then gently place Elena into her
crib. Her eyes on the sleeping infant, Lucy backed
carefully away.

His eyes remained on Lucy. On the blouse she
had not bothered to close. Annoyed with his lack

of control, Dylan upbraided himself as he turned away just as she reached him.

"What's the matter?" she whispered, easing the door closed. There was a monitor on beside the crib, with a receiver tuned to it in her bedroom and another turned on in the kitchen. Lucy intended on taking no chances with this precious miracle that had happened into her life so completely by accident. "You look like you've got something on your mind."

Because he couldn't string three coherent words together when she looked like that, Dylan began closing the buttons on her blouse himself, careful not to skim his fingers along her skin.

"I was just thinking..."

Damn, why did his throat suddenly feel so dry? And why were his thoughts breaking up like so much wet tissue in a gale? It wasn't as if he hadn't seen her nude before. He had.

Maybe that was just the trouble. He knew exactly what she looked like, devoid of clothing and with the moonlight caressing her flesh. His very breath stopped in his lungs until he forced it out again.

Despite what she knew were his best efforts, she felt Dylan's fingers brush against her breast as one button eluded him. Heat instantly fanned out from the point of contact, spreading through her like wildfire in the peak of a long, dry summer. She felt her blood begin to rush through her. It took her a second to catch her breath.

"What?" she coaxed softly. "What was it you were thinking?"

As if he could actually think when she was like

this. When he wanted her like this. "Damn it, Lucy, you're making this hard."

Her smile curved along her lips slowly, like a sultry summer breeze teasing the trees. "Are you sure you want to be doing that?"

All that separated him from some gangly, stumbling adolescent was that he was twelve years older and his mouth wasn't hanging open. "Doing what?"

"Closing the buttons." She placed her hands over his, stilling them. Making them press against her. "You don't want them closed, do you?"

He shut his eyes, fighting urges, fighting needs. He wanted to be fair to her. That was all he'd ever wanted, to be fair to her, no matter how unfair it ultimately was to him.

When he opened them again, his eyes met hers. He couldn't take much more of this. This wasn't the kind of test he could successfully withstand. "Lucy, I'm only human."

"I know," she whispered. "So am I."

Something snapped within him. Or maybe it just melted. Whatever happened, his resistance fell to zero. Unable to hold himself in check any longer, Dylan swept her into his arms. With hunger battering at him relentlessly, he kissed her.

Over and over again, his mouth slanted across hers, each kiss deeper than the last, each kiss waking up greater needs. It slowly dawned on him that he was insatiable. That when it came to Lucy, he would never be at a point where he had enough.

Lips trailing along her skin, he found the hollow of her throat and tasted the sultry flavor there. Her heavy sigh and the moan that vibrated along his mouth and in his ears only ignited him further, fanning flames that were already high by any standard.

Her arms wound tightly around him, Lucy bit back the sob of pure joy and pleasure as she felt his hands pass over her body, claiming what had always been his to begin with.

She felt her body heating, dissolving to a liquid state as she pressed herself against him. Pulses throughout her body throbbed, reminding her just how much she wanted him, how much she wanted to consummate this invisible union that existed between them. That would always exist between them no matter what words she used to tell herself that it wasn't so. There was no use fighting it and she wouldn't even try any longer. Whatever transpired in her life, whatever fortunes came and went, Lucy knew she would always love Dylan.

There would never be any other man for her heart, because it was already taken.

By him.

The air hit her abruptly, freezing everything. Her eyes flew open in dazed surprise. Slowly, they focused on Dylan's face, seeing frustrated bewilderment and self-disgust in his expression. Something within her began to tremble. She couldn't bear it if he began to back away from her now.

"What?" The single word depleted all the air in her lungs.

He tried to put some distance between them and could only manage a few inches. It was as if his feet were made of lead and there was glue on the bottom of his shoes. He wanted to be here like this with her. And that was just the problem.

"Dammit, Lucy, we can't do this." He looked

at her, silently pleading for her help because he could not tear himself away from her. "*I* can't do this."

He couldn't just work her up into a fever pitch and then retreat. Could he? She'd all but given him an open invitation to take her. Someone else would have become angry, would have turned away, salvaging what there was left of their pride.

But someone else didn't love him the way she did. "Why?" she asked.

"Because—" Frustration tied his tongue into knots. "Because you're not ready. Because—"

And then she understood. He wasn't rejecting her. He wasn't thinking of himself, he was thinking of her. *Every time I'm ready to give up on you, you do something sweet. No wonder I'm so confused.*

Lucy pressed her fingers gently against his lips, silencing him. "My doctor said I made a remarkable recovery. She said my labor was so fast and I was so healthy, that I'm back to where I was before I became pregnant." She spoke low, coaxing his hands back to her waist. "I haven't made love with anyone in over nine months." Her face upturned, she smiled into his eyes. "Believe me, Dylan, I am more than ready."

Maybe, if he tried very hard, he could resist his own urges, clamp down iron gates around them and contain them somehow. But he couldn't resist her. Hadn't the strength to turn his back on what she was offering him so willingly, not when every fiber of his body wanted her.

Not when *he* wanted her.

Ever since he'd walked out on her, he'd felt as if half of his soul was missing. A soul he'd only found the very first time he made love with her. When she had shown him that making love was more than a matter of body coming to body, skin touching skin. She'd shown him that there were souls involved, and feelings that transcended the physical.

Still, uncertainty remained a haunting shadow. He didn't want to hurt her. That had been the point from the very beginning. Not hurting Lucy.

"Are you sure?" His voice sounded raspy to his own ears.

Her smile was teasing and sweet as she felt it curve her mouth. Her eyes holding his, she began to slowly unbutton his shirt, slipping one button out at a time even while she wanted to rip the shirt from his body. But this was more effective. This heightened both their desires. She could see it rising like a flame in his eyes.

A flame that found a twin within her soul.

She wanted to tempt him, to ensnare him the way he had her. Lucy knew she'd do whatever she had to do to keep him from backing away again. She couldn't bear it if he turned away from her now, not when she wanted him so. Needed him so.

Rising on her toes, her lips a scant breath away from his, she whispered, "Very sure."

The last thread of his fraying resistance gave way, snapping. It took supreme effort and control on his part not to take her then and there, not to devour her with his mouth and plunge himself into her the way the demands slamming through his body urged him to.

He wanted so badly to lose himself within her sweetness, to forget who and what he was. To forget his destiny and the demons that hovered over him, waiting for that one unguarded moment when they could slip through and take possession of him.

Eagerness seemed to radiate all through him, pulsating in every part of his body. His hands, his mouth, his limbs. Reining himself in as much as he could, Dylan forced himself to go slowly.

Even as the madness threatened to take over, he knew he wouldn't hurt Lucy for the world.

As his lips found hers again, and his hands worshiped her body, divesting her of her clothing, he felt something moist along her cheek. Drawing his head back, he saw the shadow of tears staining her skin.

Dammit, he *was* hurting her, he upbraided himself angrily.

"Just something in my eye," she murmured.

And then, her fingers tangling in his hair, she brought his mouth back to hers. Not for the world would she tell him that they were tears of happiness. That for this one shining moment, they were together again and she was undyingly glad of it. She didn't want to frighten him away.

Optimistic to a fault, she had still become too much the realist to believe that what was between them this moment could last forever. He didn't want it to. But it existed now and that was as much as she could hope for.

There were no guarantees in life. There were only moments to be seized and savored.

And remembered.

Like now.

When he felt her long, graceful fingers brush along his belly, tugging away at his belt, every sinew within him tightened, threatening to snap apart like so many dry strands of spaghetti.

Did she have any idea what she was doing to him, how much control he was exercising not to ravage her here and now? He doubted it.

Dylan caught his breath, his blood pumping wildly as she nipped at his throat, her hands slipping along his hips, moving his jeans and his underwear down simultaneously. He gripped her buttocks, kneading them, his thumbs forming light semicircles along her flesh. She leaned into him, arching her back, driving him up to the very apex of insanity.

He pulled himself back from the brink, though there was no way to decelerate the speed with which his heart was hammering. His body burned where she had touched it, undressing him. His body burned to be touched by her. All of her.

If he had thought of it, he would have carried her to the bed, but he didn't think of it. All he could manage to do was to sink down to his knees, worshiping the woman fate had brought back to him a second time.

Brought back to taunt him and tantalize him with what he couldn't ultimately have.

But that was for later.

He had now. And now was all he could hope for.

His fingers linked with hers, he brought her down to the floor, every micro-inch marked with hot, searing, openmouthed kisses.

And then he was over her. Looking into those eyes of hers that held his soul. Hands still joined above her head, he lowered himself slowly into her.

And found the other half of his soul waiting for him, just where he had left it.

The ride was sweet, swift, consuming, and when it was over and they were spent, he held her in his arms and prayed for forever.

And absolution for what he'd just done. It would make the leaving that much more difficult for both of them. Most assuredly for him.

Chapter 13

Guilt came, strong and hard, nudging aside the soothing feeling of peace until it disappeared altogether. Damn him, anyway. It wasn't just her physical condition he should have been mindful of, he upbraided himself, it was her emotional one as well. She was alone, deserted by her lover, deprived of the brother she loved, a new mother faced with challenges everywhere she turned. And some maniac who had broken into her home and her store was still out there on the loose.

And he had complicated things by bringing her back to a place they had inhabited a year ago. A place they couldn't remain.

What the hell was the matter with him? Why couldn't he get a better grip on himself?

All he could do was ask her forgiveness. He'd never asked anyone's forgiveness before. The words tangled on his tongue and stuck to one another, refusing to form coherently.

"Lucy," he began slowly, his tone warning her that they were drifting back to where they'd been a few short hours ago. "I didn't mean for this to happen."

Lying beside him on the floor, Lucy wanted to hang on to the euphoria, the magic just a little longer. Surely he couldn't deprive her of that. Slowly, she turned into him and looked up at his face.

"You start apologizing to me now, Detective McMorrow, and your police buddies are going to have to come here and book me on charges of justifiable homicide." Humor quirked her mouth as she rose up on her elbow. "No court in the world would convict me."

Her dark hair was brushing along her breast, not quite covering the swell. Tempting him all over again. Dylan groaned, hating his weakness.

Loving her.

"Not if you go in front of them like that," he agreed. Hungry for her all over again, surrendering to the inevitable, he cupped the back of her head and brought her mouth to his.

He meant only to savor just one more kiss fleetingly. One more for the road. The long, winding road that would lead him away from her.

When Lucy turned into him, her body sealing to his, he knew he was lying to himself again.

He'd been lying to himself all along, thinking he could be counted among the living. It was only when he was with Lucy, when he breathed in the scent of her hair, when he touched her face, when he looked at her the way he was looking at her now that he was truly alive.

Or even wanted to be.

Urges hammering at him, Dylan gave up the pretense that once was enough. A thousand times would not be enough if he had to ultimately go on without her. He knew he would be faced with that all too soon because even as he held her against him, even as he surrendered himself to the desires that were vibrating, large, whole and demanding, between them, he knew that he was going to have to walk away from her again.

Nothing had changed that. The only thing that would change is that this time, it was going to be even harder than before. Because this time, he was not only in love with her, but with her daughter as well.

He hadn't thought that the hole he bore in his heart could be any larger than it was, but he had been wrong.

But he wasn't going to think about that now, not when the night loomed, dark and endless, before him and she was so willing in his arms.

He murmured her name against her mouth as he took her to where there was only room for the two of them, with no thoughts of tomorrow, no regrets of today. He made love to every inch of her with every inch of himself. It was little enough, he felt, that he could give her.

The shrill ringing noise by his head jarred him into wakefulness. A second later, Dylan recognized the sound. Lucy's bedroom telephone was ringing. Suddenly alert, Dylan snapped up into a sitting position, reaching for the receiver even as something warm stirred against him.

Warm sensations traveled over the length of his body as he remembered where he was. Last night returned to him with crystal clarity.

He didn't want to be answering a telephone, he wanted to be making love with Lucy all over again. No doubt about it, he thought, the woman was highly addictive. But it was an addiction he would have gladly lived with had circumstances been different.

Dragging his hand through his hair, wiping away the last remnants of sleep, he barked a ''hello'' into the receiver, then took a sharp breath as he felt her hand creep up on his thigh. Desire came, unannounced but not unexpected. He covered her hand with his, listening to the voice on the other end of the line.

''Your cell phone's dead,'' Watley told him. There was a tinge of exasperation in his voice. ''I've been trying to reach you for over half an hour. You forget to charge it again?''

''Yeah.'' Dylan looked down at Lucy, curled up against him, her hair still partially in her face. He'd forgotten a lot of things last night. Like where he was supposed to tread. He blew out a breath, trying to focus his mind. ''What time is it?''

''That depends on who you are.''

Riddles. Watley had more annoying habits… Dylan felt impatience beginning to nibble away at him. He looked at his wristwatch, the only thing he hadn't taken off last night.

''Watley, it's five past six in the morning. It's

too early for one of your damn puzzles. What the hell do you mean, that depends on who you are?''

There was a weariness in Watley's voice that sheer lack of sleep couldn't bring about. ''That time stands still when you're dead.''

His partner had his full attention now. Beside him, Lucy was sitting up. Dylan could feel her eyes on him, a silent question in them.

''Who's dead?'' he asked Watley.

''Michelson.'' It was the accountant who had approached them, offering what they had hoped was their first solid lead. ''Two joggers found a decomposing body this morning in Heritage Park.''

Ritchie's body had been found not a mile away from his home. Heritage Park was all the way over on the other side of town. The killers got around, Dylan thought grimly. So much for hoping Michelson had run off to another country and could still be tracked down.

''Are they sure?''

''He still had his college ring on. The guys at the medical examiner's office are confirming his ID even as we speak. Alexander tracked down Michelson's dentist and got his dental records.''

Two murders. The man they were after wasn't afraid of killing to cover his trail. He'd been right to have Lucy guarded. ''Where are you?''

''Right now, I'm at the coroner's office, but I'm on my way out. I'll meet you at the station whenever you feel you can tear yourself away. Captain wants to hold a meeting. And McMorrow—''

Dylan swung his legs out over the side of the bed, looking around for his pants. He remembered that they were out in the hall, along with the rest of his clothes. And hers. "Yeah?"

"Charge your damn phone, will you? I had to waste time, calling around to get this number. Your lady friend isn't listed."

"That's 'cause she's smart."

Dylan hung up the receiver. Lady friend, he thought. As if the term could even begin to describe what Lucy was to him. Turning toward her, he discovered that Lucy was already out of bed and, for the most part, dressed. He knew there was no underwear beneath the clothes she'd shrugged on and the knowledge went a long way toward undermining the rest of his thoughts.

There was concern mingled with understanding in her eyes. She'd found his jeans and brought them back into the room for him. "You have to go?"

"Yeah. Lucy—"

There were a thousand things he wanted to tell her, but he couldn't wrap his tongue around a single coherent thought. All he could say was her name and let it linger in the air between them.

She heard the quandary in his voice, the hesitation. He was regretting last night already, regretting it because he was afraid that she might think it was opening the door to something. She didn't feel up to telling him that she knew it wasn't, that she knew nothing had changed. Not the way he felt, not the way she felt. But it had been a beautiful night and she didn't want to spoil it now.

"Then I'd better get you some coffee."

Flashing a quick smile as she tossed him his shirt, Lucy hurried from the room.

* * *

The image of her standing in the doorway, with Elena in her arms, kept replaying itself over and over in his head as he drove to the station. If he had worried about her because of Ritchie's murder, he was doubly so now that the accountant had been found. But without any hard evidence, it was difficult to get anyone in an official capacity within the department to authorize round-the-clock protection for her.

He'd called Reed and asked him if he'd mind taking her to work. The man had told him not to worry. But Dylan was worried. Dylan knew this tag-team security system couldn't go on indefinitely.

Dylan turned off the thoroughfare, taking the street that eventually led him to the police department's main building. Maybe he was too close to all this to realize that the danger might be more imagined on his part than real.

There was no maybe about it, at least as far as being too close to the situation went. Even before he'd slept with Lucy last night, he'd done exactly what he always schooled himself not to do. He had lost his professional perspective.

He'd lost a lot of things when it came to Lucy, he thought. The piece of tin he called his heart, for starters.

Dylan forced himself to push thoughts of Lucy out of his head as he hurried up the stone steps leading into the modern-looking building that housed the precinct.

The meeting was brief.

Dental records had indeed confirmed the man's

identity. The Den of Thieves' lost accountant was no longer lost. But what was lost was their edge and the inside information they had still been banking on.

"So, where does this leave us?" Dylan wondered out loud after the captain had finished his briefing. He looked around at the three other men seated around the small conference table, all the men on the surveillance detail. Two men off regular detail were covering for them for the duration of the meeting.

The captain cleared his throat. Newly transferred to his position, he appeared none-too-happy about the slow progression of events. "With a lot of video footage of the front of the restaurant, hearsay from a witness who can no longer raise his right hand to swear to tell the truth, so help him God, and not much else."

"What about Romano?" Alexander, who along with Hathaway made up one half of the other surveillance team that had been drafted, asked about their man on the inside. "Hasn't he gotten anything?"

Dylan had been out of touch the last half of yesterday. He listened for the answer, thinking the news couldn't continue to be this bleak. With an inward start, he realized that Lucy's optimism had to be rubbing off on him. There was no other reason for him to believe that the news could be anything *but* bleak.

"Yeah, a rash from the wire he's been wearing," Watley quipped in frustration.

The captain looked as disgusted as the rest of them. It was obvious to his men that he didn't take having egg on his face well. "It looks like we might have to pack it in as far as the investigation goes."

A murmur of protest met his words.

"We can't quit now," Dylan told his superior.

The captain nodded toward Dylan's partner. "Watley's unfinished puzzle notwithstanding, we're putting in too many man hours on this and it's leading nowhere. The commissioner feels we can better use our efforts elsewhere."

Dylan felt otherwise. They had put in too much time to back off now. "It's not like Bedford's a hotbed of crime," he pointed out. "We're not pulling men away from other, more pressing investigations. Can't you get us a little more time?"

The captain tugged on his chin, debating siding with his men or standing against them with his superiors. But Dylan was right. Bedford was growing by leaps and bounds and although it no longer was the sleepy-eyed, three light town it had been twenty some odd years ago, crime in Bedford usually meant tools stolen from a shed or a bicycle absconded from a driveway. To have a place like Den of Thieves in their midst, where money was being laundered with only a semblance of an attempt to hide the fact, was a disgrace and a blot on all their names.

The captain looked at the four men sitting before him. "Okay, we've got the accountant coming forward with what he says was some kind of evidence and he gets killed for it." He looked at Dylan. "You say Ritchie Alvarez probably had something on Palmero and he gets killed for it. In my book that says there's something going on here, something we can't just walk away from."

There was silence in the room as the captain debated the course to be followed. "All right, we'll sink a few more days into it. If nothing comes up in a week, I won't have a choice. I'll have to close the operation down." It was clear that he didn't want to do that. "See if one of you can bring me Palmero's head on a platter before then. I'd consider it an early Christmas present." He looked around him at the men. "Well, get going."

Chairs scraped against the newly installed flooring as they were returned to their places and the detectives prepared to return to theirs.

"Did I interrupt anything?" Watley asked, hurrying after Dylan as they left the room.

Dylan slanted a look at the other man as he stopped by the coffee machine. The coffee was notoriously bad, but it was better than nothing. Digging into his pocket, he looked for change. Not finding any, he took a dollar and stuffed it into the empty coffee can before picking up the half-filled pot. "What are you talking about?"

Rather than coffee, Watley availed himself of the pot of hot water on the other burner. Dipping into his shirt pocket, he took out a gold-foil envelope. As Dylan watched him from beneath hooded lids, Watley stripped the foil away to expose a tea bag, which he promptly popped into a cup.

"This morning. You sounded breathless when you answered."

Dylan purposely ignored the knowing expression on his partner's face. Instead, he pretended to concentrate on the semiblack liquid pouring out of the pot into the mug he kept at the precinct. "I wasn't expecting a phone call at dawn."

Watley grinned, tossing out the used tea bag. "Obviously," he commented, then backed off. "Did you charge your cell phone?"

Exasperation creased Dylan's forehead. He'd never been one for questions. It reminded him too much of interrogations he'd gone through as a kid, interrogations his father conducted because he enjoyed making him sweat. Once Dylan had picked up on that, he refused to show his father any emotion whatsoever. That was when the beatings were stepped up.

"What are you, my keeper?" He bit back his annoyance, cooling off. "Yeah, I charged it." Plugging the phone into the portable charger, he'd given the battery a quick dose while he showered.

Watley's grin spread, but there was gentle humor in his eyes. "What else did you charge?"

Dylan knew the baiting was harmless, but he still wasn't in the mood for it. Because it was his partner, he went easier on him than he might have. "Back off, Watley, or Michelson's not the only one they're going to be sending dental charts for."

Laughing, Watley set down his empty mug and shook his head. "Don't know what that woman sees in you. I guess her tastes run to Neanderthal types."

Dylan looked at his watch, not for the first time, and wondered if Reed had taken Lucy to the shop yet. She should be there by now.

"She doesn't see anything in me." Watley was still grinning at him. "And can we keep my personal life out of this?"

"Speaking of which, the desk sergeant asked me to give you these," Watley said. Digging into his inside jacket pocket, Watley pulled out a wad of blue pages. Each paper represented a message the sergeant had taken for Dylan.

Taking them, Dylan stared at the pieces of paper in silence. They were each from the same person. His father. Raising his eyes, he saw that Watley had already made the same discovery.

"I'd say for a man who was dead, he's being pretty persistent."

The word *urgent* underlined several times jumped out at him before he shoved the messages into his back pocket. "No one asked you to say anything."

"I'm generous that way," Watley quipped. Then the smile faded a little as he grew serious. "Why don't you call him? Or better yet, go see him." Dylan gave him a dark look that warned him to back off. "Hey, whatever's between the two of you needs clearing up."

Dylan thought better of the retort that rose to his lips. For all his hounding and heavy-handedness, Watley meant well. "You've been listening to that radio shrink again, haven't you?"

Watley shook his head. Because Dylan was already walking away, he hurried to catch up.

"No, this is from personal experience. I didn't talk to my old man for five years. Some blowup, I don't even remember about what anymore. Point is, I faced him, got things squared away. Now we talk maybe once a week, sometimes more. He's turned into a decent guy. Maybe your old man has, too."

That could work for some people, but not for Dylan and not for the man who had made his life a living hell for too many years.

"Not unless you believe in miracles." He thought of his mother and shook his head. She'd gone on hoping his father would change until the day she died. It was the misery his father had brought into his mother's life that Dylan couldn't forgive the man for. "Besides, it's too late for that."

"It's never too late," Watley told him. "Not while both of you are breathing."

Dylan curbed the impulse to tell Watley to get off his back. "I've used up all my personal time."

"Since when?" Watley hooted. "Until this case came up, you amassed enough time to send the entire department on a two-week vacation. Hell, McMorrow, you never take any time off. People are beginning to think you're part of the furniture."

Dylan walked outside, holding the door open for Watley. He glanced at his partner, debating. There had been more than ten messages in the last two days. Curiosity rubbed at him, leaving a small dent in its wake.

"Your wife ever get a chance to do any talking when you're home?"

Following him down the stairs to where their vehicles were parked, Watley laughed. "Why do you think I talk so much when I'm around you? She never lets me get a word in edgewise. Once the baby's born, I may even forget how to talk altogether."

Dylan laughed shortly. "I should be so lucky."

"Why don't you go see him?" Watley urged. "Be the bigger man. If he's anything like you, you'll both grunt at each other and you'll be at the stakeout before I get there." He opened his car door. "You know where to find him?"

Same place he had been for the last forty years, Dylan thought. "Yeah, I know where to find him."

But he didn't.

When Dylan arrived at the house where he'd grown up, there was no one to answer his knock. For a moment, he stood on the sagging front porch, telling himself he was crazy to come back. That this was pointless. Hadn't he sworn never to set foot in the house again?

Dylan shifted and the wood beneath his boots groaned loudly. Or was that the echo of childish groans from years gone by?

There were demons here, he thought, demons he had fled. Demons he realized he needed to face now so that he could continue on with his life, such as it was. Making a decision, he used the key he had kept for reasons that were beyond his own comprehension and let himself in.

He was assaulted with a barrage of memories the second he walked into the airless, dusty house. For a moment, it felt as if he couldn't breathe, his throat closing as he struggled with feelings he didn't want to deal with. Telling himself that he was a grown man, that what had happened within these walls could no longer touch him, he still struggled to make his way quickly through the one-story structure.

"You here, old man?"

But there was no one to answer his call. Passing through the rooms, he satisfied himself that his father was nowhere on the premises. Well, he'd tried.

Which was a hell of a lot more than his father had ever done, even in the best of times.

Walking out again, he pulled the door firmly shut behind him, as if to keep the memories from leaking out and onto him. He was almost to the curb and his car when he heard his name being called.

"Dylan, is that you?"

He turned at the sound of the reedy voice and saw a thin woman squinting at him from the porch of the house next door. Recognition set in. He remembered thinking the woman looked old when he was a child. She seemed to have remained the same. Only he had aged.

Giving himself a little more time, he stepped away from the curb. "Hello, Mrs. Olsen. Yes, it's me."

Obviously pleased to see him, the old woman bustled over, her eager smile erasing some of the wrinkles on her face instead of emphasizing them.

In the manner of an adult with a child she hadn't see for a long time, Mrs. Olsen was quick to take his hands in hers. "Let me take a look at you, it's been such a long time."

The woman, a widow ever since he could remember, had been friendly with his mother. In deference to that, Dylan stood still for the scrutiny she subjected him to even when all he wanted was to leave.

Alice Olsen nodded with approval. "You've turned out to be a fine, handsome young man, Dylan. Always knew you would. Look like her, you do." She sighed, patting his arm, remembering his mother with fondness. "Did you come looking for your father?"

The denial was a reflex, but he suppressed it. "Yes, you can tell him I came by." With that, he turned to leave.

"He's in the hospital, you know," she called after him. "The ambulance came and took him away just before eight o'clock last night."

Dylan turned slowly around.

Chapter 14

The corridors didn't smell of antiseptic, not even faintly. That surprised him. He'd always associated hospitals and the sick with antiseptic.

Dylan stood outside the third-floor hospital room, his hands in his pockets, wondering what he was doing here. The intensive-care-unit beds were all full, the fresh-faced receptionist at the first-floor information desk had told him, so his father had been placed here, in the surgical care section. Harry McMorrow's condition was serious and he was deteriorating fast. There wasn't anything anyone could do but wait.

Twice on the twenty-mile drive over to Harris Memorial, Dylan had almost stopped and turned his car around. Yet somehow, he hadn't. He'd continued. And now he was here, standing outside his father's hospital room, still not certain why he came, still not certain if he should even bother going in or not.

The man on the other side of the door was his father only in the strictest dictionary, biological sense of the word. There was nothing about Harry McMorrow that remotely made him a father the way greeting cards and sentimental dramas envisioned fathers to be. There had never been any long talks where wisdom had been handed down from one generation to the next, or moments to treasure and remember. On the contrary, to Dylan's complete recollection, Harry McMorrow had never been anything but cold, self-centered and controlling. He had kept his wife and his son on short emotional leashes every day of their collective lives together.

When he had become old enough to understand and make his own judgments, Dylan had strained against the tether his father had wound around him. His father had tried to beat the willfulness out of him. Instead of breaking his spirit, the beatings only made it stronger, made his resolve stronger until he'd finally run away. More than anything, he'd wanted to take his mother with him, to save her. But she had been too afraid to leave the only man she had ever been with.

This was, she'd told him over and over again, the way life was supposed to be. One life, one man. And she wound up giving her life to her husband because eventually, he'd killed her. Not with a single blow or a single incident, but he'd killed her spirit, her laughter and her promise until she had finally given up her will to live.

It was all that and more that he held against his father.

Remembering, Dylan told himself that he was a fool to have come, to be here now, wavering before the door of a man he had once deemed a monster.

Maybe it was the cop in him, wanting to know why, after all this time, the man who had never loved him was asking so insistently to see him. He'd never mattered to his father before.

Some ingrained instinct of survival had Dylan passing his hand over his gun, hidden beneath his jacket, as he walked into the room.

Sunlight had made itself at home in every corner, its rays adding a ghostly cheeriness to the room as they rested along the frame of a man who was no longer robust, no longer a threat except in memory.

For a second, as he looked at the sleeping shell of a man, Dylan thought he'd made a mistake and entered the wrong room. The emaciated figure, almost lost within his bedclothes, bore little resemblance to the man who had stood at Dylan's mother's grave site ten years ago, contemptuously egging him on to fight, one last time, for his mother's honor.

He'd been too full of sorrow and loss to raise a hand then, though a part of him had wanted to. But no blows, no victory would have brought his mother back. So he had turned his back on his father and walked away. A flurry of vile names had followed him out of the cemetery.

The man in the bed looked almost a hundred pounds lighter than that man at the cemetery had. There were tubes crisscrossed over him, like Scotch tape that had come loose from a gift that had been tossed aside and overlooked. His hands, once so powerful and threatening, now seemed weak and lifeless, lying on top of the blanket as if someone had posed them there as an afterthought.

Lids that were almost translucent fluttered, then opened. Watery pale blue eyes stared at him in stony silence. Dylan wondered if his father even recognized him.

"Hello, old man."

The cracked, parched lips parted, emitting a harsh, raspy sound. The tubes in his nose mitigated a once-powerful baritone, reducing it to a rattling whisper. "You came."

"Yeah, I came." There was so much to say and nothing to say. Years of unspoken questions jumbled in Dylan's brain, all demanding to be asked at once. He gave voice to the most immediate one. "Why are you calling me?"

A reedy, thin hand, the same hand that had once pummeled him, the same hand that had shoved him, screaming, into a closet and locked the door, leaving him there for hours to deal with the dark and his terror, barely lifted up from the bed in a hopeless gesture. It fell back, pressed down by the weight of the plastic tube attached to it.

"I wanted to see you."

That begged more questions than it answered. "Why?"

His father struggled to push the words out. "To tell you...to tell you... I'm sorry." As he spoke, moisture trickled from the corner of his eye, sliding down toward his ear.

Crocodile tears, Dylan thought, shed by a crocodile. He wasn't taken in. "I don't need your apology, old man."

A faded spark that could have once been anger

glimmered for a fleeting moment in Harry's eyes, then disappeared.

"But I need to give it. To ask…"

Even now, he couldn't say it, Dylan thought cynically. His father couldn't ask to be forgiven. That was what he was after, absolution. Before he met his Maker. It looked as if his father's two-pack-a-day habit had finally caught up with him. Funny how a leafy plant could lay him low while destroying the life of a good woman had had no effect on the man.

"To ask for what?" Dylan prodded. "Forgiveness? Why, because you're dying?"

The fight, always so omnipresent in his father's countenance, had been drained out as the poisons that were shutting down his system had spread. The air he sucked into his lungs rattled there. "Yes."

Dylan's eyes narrowed. "I'm not Mom."

"But you have her eyes…. And her smile." More tears followed the first, sliding faster down the trail that had been forged. "Your mother was a beautiful woman, once."

"You killed that, just like you killed everything else."

A sob escaped the cracked lips. "I know. I couldn't help it. God, I am sorry, but I couldn't help it." Harry raised his hand again, reaching for his son. He grasped only air. "You have to believe me."

"You could have helped it, old man."

Dylan wanted to hate him, the way he had hated him all these years. But he couldn't. Instead, he felt the anger and contempt he had come armed with being nudged aside by pity. He could almost hear his mother whispering in his ear, the way she had countless times when she had been alive, asking him to forgive his father because he "didn't mean it." *He needs our understanding, Dylan, not our hate.* "You could have tried to *get* help."

"You're right." The man began to sob in earnest, his body fairly shaking with the sound.

Poetic justice would have had him walking away without a backward glance. But Dylan discovered that, after all this time, he was still too much his mother's son to do it. Vengeance was a hollow thing. It served no purpose to walk away, withholding the one thing the man wanted from him. The triumph would have been empty, the victory without celebration. It wouldn't be avenging his mother, who was years past gaining any benefit from it.

Extracting vengeance would have made him, Dylan realized, as little a man as his father had been. With a sigh, Dylan gave the old man what he wanted and cleared him from his conscience.

He took the hand that had found only air seeking his, and held it. The watery eyes refocused, a pathetic gratitude shimmering in them as Harry looked up at him. "I forgive you, old man. You'll have a higher court than me to face pretty soon."

In place of a reply, his father began to cough. The cough racked him, threatening to rip out all the tubes that were in him. Dylan drew his father into a sitting position, afraid he would choke. He was surprised at how paper-thin and frail the man actually felt.

When the fit finally subsided, Harry sighed with relief and exhaustion. Dylan lowered his father back against his pillow. Harry held on as tightly as he could to his hand. "Stay with me?"

Dylan thought of Lucy. A call to the shop on his cell phone had assuaged his concern. Lucy and Elena had arrived right on schedule and were fine. Watley had promised to cover for him at the surveillance, telling him to take all the time he needed. As usual, there was nothing doing at the restaurant. If there were any illegal transactions going on, they were so covert that they remained undetected.

Dylan wrestled with his conscience. His conscience won, even though the man in the bed had done nothing to merit an ounce of charity. But his mother would have wanted it this way. It was for her, not his father, that he remained.

"Okay." Still holding the emaciated hand, Dylan pulled over a chair and sat down beside the old man.

He hadn't said a word to her.

The entire trip home from the shop had been marked with his stony silence. Beyond a faint noise Lucy took as a grunt, Dylan hadn't responded to any of her attempts to get a conversation going between them, or at least some sort of acknowledgment. It made her uneasy.

Dylan had walked into the shop at the usual time and stood, like some inanimate, godlike clone, waiting for her to get Elena and come home with him. The only response he'd made to Alma's bantered greeting was to look in her direction. Nothing more.

Now, sitting beside him in the car with her baby dozing in the back, Lucy came to the only conclusion she could. He was leaving. The thought brought a sudden sharp chill that passed over her, scraping clammy nails along her body. Twisting her heart.

Well, if he was leaving again, he was going to have to do better than this in letting her know. She turned in her seat to face him. "If you're auditioning for a stone statue, you won the part hands down."

Dylan glanced in her direction, then looked back at the road. They had almost reached her house.

She didn't know how much more of this she could stand. "You're carrying this strong, silent type bit too far, don't you think?"

Still he said nothing and she blew out an angry breath. Ten months ago, she might have remained quiet, but she had done a lot of growing up since then. They were going to have this out like adults. She wanted to know what had caused this complete withdrawal after they had come so far last night and this morning. She refused to believe he was just being perverse.

"Look, if you think that I've done something, I want to know what it is. Tell me," she insisted.

"You haven't done anything."

Her hand flew to her chest. "He speaks, be still my heart." And then the semismile faded from her lips. "All right, if *you've* done something, tell me that, too. I have a right to know why you suddenly have become a complete mute. This is quiet, even for you."

Dylan pulled into her driveway and yanked up the hand brake before cutting off the engine. He didn't want to tell her, didn't want to talk about it.

Maybe if he ignored it, what had happened today would just evaporate from his memory.

But he knew there was little chance of that. The emotions that were churning within him threatened to push the walls of his dam too hard, breaking them down. Dylan got out and slammed the door on his side a little too firmly. The jarring noise woke Elena out of her dozing state. He cursed himself for his oversight.

"I saw my father today."

Lucy had gotten out of the car and was unstrapping Elena. She gave no indication that the information startled her. She'd been sure he was going to continue to ignore the other man. Taking the baby out and holding her, Lucy looked at him. "And?"

The image of his father lying in the hospital came back to him. He tried to shut it out. "He's dying."

"Oh, Dylan, I'm sorry." Lucy quickly rounded the hood to reach him.

He saw the sympathy in her eyes. His face hardened. "Don't be. He deserves to die."

Without another word, he took Elena from her and strode into the house. Stunned, she stared at his back before hurrying in after him.

"What are you doing?"

He didn't even bother turning around. Instead, he walked toward the rear of the house and the nursery. "She needs to be changed."

Watching him disappear, Lucy felt as if her limbs weren't quite solid. If there had been a breeze passing through the house, she was certain she probably would have fallen over. Biting her lower lip, she began to follow, then forced herself to remain where she was.

Maybe after what he'd just been through, Dylan needed this time alone with a brand-new, shiny life. Needed the baby to help make him feel whole again. She accepted the fact that being with Elena right now could help him the way she couldn't.

Lucy smiled to herself. At the very least, Elena wouldn't ask him any questions he didn't want to answer.

With a resigned sigh, Lucy retreated. She went into the kitchen to attempt to do something useful while she waited for Dylan to come out of the nursery again.

It was a long wait.

She tried talking to him again after dinner. "I know you're not given to talking."

Dylan silently raised his eyebrow at her as she cleared away the plate in front of him. He'd hardly eaten anything, even when she'd urged food on him. In desperation, Lucy had turned on the radio to fill in the silence. It hadn't really helped. She wanted to hear the sound of his voice. She wanted him to share with her whatever it was that was bothering him.

The man was infuriating, but she loved him and she wanted to help.

When there was no more response forthcoming than his raised eyebrow, she stood looking at him. "I've gotten more conversation out of teakettles than you, but if you do want to talk, I'm here."

Dylan looked away, wishing she would back off. He'd felt pity for that shriveled old man today. Pity, dammit. He didn't want to feel anything but hatred, to acknowledge anything but contempt. Pity opened up other emotions. Pity weakened him and ate away at his defenses. "I don't want to talk."

Lucy felt like hurling the dishes she was holding against the wall to make him sit up and take notice. She was trying to open up lines of communication and he kept applying wire cutters to them. With effort, she restrained the exasperation she felt and tried again.

"Don't you think you should?" She laid a hand on his shoulder. "It's obviously eating at you, this thing about your father."

He shrugged it away, missing the look of pain that came into her eyes. "I can deal with it on my own."

When he turned away, she put herself squarely before him again, lowering her face to his. "But you don't have to. Don't you see that? You *don't* have to. You can talk to me." What did it take to break through that damn shell of his? "Everyone needs to talk."

"I don't."

"Yes," she insisted, getting in his face again when he tried to turn from her. "You do." She intended to keep getting in his face until he finally talked to her. "You need to get whatever's bothering you out. Don't you understand? It's a poison, and if you don't get it out, it's going to keep on festering inside of you until it destroys you." Her eyes narrowed, pinning him. "Until you become some bitter old man who hates the world."

She'd used the exact same phrasing he had once flung at his father. It had earned him a split lip and a mouth full of blood. Dylan resented the comparison. Resented more the reality that he could easily turn into his father.

Turn into everything he had hated for so long.

Well, wasn't that why he had left Lucy to begin with? Because he was afraid that he would turn into his father? That he would wind up hurting and destroying the very person he loved more than life itself?

Disgusted, he rose abruptly from his chair. It toppled over. Dylan ignored it, trying to get away from her. Away from what she was saying. "You don't know what you're talking about."

But she was there, in front of him again, her chin raised like a tempting target, her eyes blazing. Giving him no peace.

"Then tell me," she demanded. "Tell me what I'm talking about." The anger at his stubborn refusal faded a little, softening as she added, "Please."

He couldn't resist her.

Not when she lay herself bare like this before him. Not when she seemed so determined to absorb the pain that was eating away at him so that he could be free of it.

"Dammit, woman, why won't you back off when I tell you to?"

"Because I love you."

The words broke him. "Dammit, Lucy, you don't know what you're saying." Cursing the empty shell that had once been his soul, Dylan roughly framed her face and pulled her to him, sealing his mouth to hers.

Emotions spun wildly through her as she felt the despair, tasted the need, the desperation that was taking hold of him. She did what she could to assuage it while her own needs battered relentlessly at her.

Needing to come up for air, Lucy sighed against his lips. He wasn't going to tell her anything, she knew that.

Her body already heating, her arms entwined around his neck, she look up at him. "Well, I guess that's communication. Of a sort."

She kept finding a way to get through no matter how hard he tried to block her way. And right now, his defenses were far too tattered and frayed to offer any resistance. Dylan rested his chin against the top of her head. "Anyone ever tell you that you talk too much?"

"You," she murmured. She could feel his heart hammering against her cheek. It filled her with a warmth that nothing else could. "All the time."

With his crooked finger beneath her chin, Dylan raised her head so that she could look at him. "Then why don't you listen?"

The soft smile crinkled the corners of her eyes. "I'm forgetful."

He looked at her then, startling her with the entreaty she saw in his eyes. "Make me forget, Lucy. Just for tonight, make me forget about everything else."

Her heart quickened, going out to him. Lucy tightened her arms around him, wishing with all her soul that she could erase the pain she saw within him. That she could somehow magically take away all the things he had lived through that had made him the isolated man he was today.

But all she could do was give him her body.

And her love.

"I'll do my best."

Her best was good enough.

Once started, the lovemaking was fast and furious, mimicking a flaming string attached to explosives that swiftly burned toward its final destination.

He wanted to feel the rapture. He wanted to savor the road.

Unable to contain himself, Dylan stripped her quickly of her clothes, almost spinning her around to get her out of them. He needed to feel her body against his, to touch it and lose himself in the reality of her flesh, her softness. He needed, more than anything else, the innocence she brought to him. The goodness. It helped to cleanse him and smother the pain that shouldn't have been there, but was.

His lips and fingertips anointed and shared every part of her, discovering her as if she were a new treasure, returning to her as if she were the only haven in a world grown cold.

Her motions mirrored his ardor as she yanked off his shirt and then pulled his jeans from his taut, hard body.

Each movement—his, hers, theirs—only served to heighten the excitement pulsing between them and infused the demands vibrating within their bodies by underscoring their anticipation.

Lucy could have sworn she felt herself almost peaking just from the way Dylan looked at her, just from the way he wanted her.

He'd never made love with her this way before, with an urgency that was breathtaking. He made love with her as if tomorrow was going to go up in flames and they had only moments left of today.

But even in his hunger, his roughness had a gentleness to it. He didn't want to hurt her, and that excited her almost more than anything else. That even now, when his soul was so obviously troubled, when he was just telling himself he was seeking solace of the body, he put her needs ahead of his own.

For all this and more, she loved him. And it would be this gentleness in the eye of the hurricane of passion that she would remember.

Remember when he was gone.

Chapter 15

Morning peered in, scattering sunshine like so many rose petals throughout the room.

It had nothing on the sunshine she felt pervading throughout her entire body. She'd been awake for a while now. Raising herself up on her elbow, Lucy smiled as she continued to watch Dylan. He was sleeping beside her, the way he once had before the world had turned ugly and she'd had to forsake some of her optimism.

Several times during the night, she'd gotten up to tend to Elena. Each time she returned, she'd found Dylan awake and waiting for her. Waiting to re-create what they had shared on the kitchen floor. Made love with wild, passionate abandon. And each time, there was a little less abandon, a little more tenderness.

She resisted the urge to run her fingers through his hair. She loved watching him sleep. His face was devoid of the tension that so often made his profile rigid, his expression unapproachable. Relaxed, he made her think of the boy she knew in her heart still existed somewhere inside.

If she hadn't already been in love with him, she would have fallen in love now.

"Is this the part where you start interrogating me?" His eyes opened to look up at her. She might have known.

"I thought you were asleep."

He'd woken up hungry for her again and awed by the thought that he really couldn't seem to get enough of her. Why was that? He'd always been satisfied with so little, why was having her never enough, only creating a need to have more?

Dylan toyed with the ribbon that held the front of her nightgown together and toyed with the notion of making love with her again before breakfast. "Haven't you heard? Cops never really sleep, they just pretend."

She laughed softly, unable to resist kissing his forehead. He tasted of sweat. And lovemaking. "Maybe that's where Elena got it from."

He felt her freeze against him, the movement registering subconsciously even as he explored her words, trying to make sense of them. "What do you mean?"

How could she have let that slip out like that? Dammit, this wasn't the way she'd wanted to let him know.

She'd begun to realize, after watching Dylan with Elena these last few weeks, that not letting him know he was the baby's father was wrong. That he needed to know. But she hadn't given up her feelings about the weight of her words. She didn't want Elena to be the reason he remained with her. She had to have his love first.

At a loss, Lucy searched for words to cover her slip, but nothing plausible occurred to her. There were already so many lies, so many denials between them, she didn't want to add to their number.

But she didn't want the truth coming to him when she was so unprepared.

When she gave him no reply, suspicions began to form. From the recesses of his mind, he remembered her saying she hadn't made love in over nine months. He hadn't paid attention then, he did now. Ten months ago, she'd been with him, not some phantom lover.

She'd deliberately lied to him.

A bitter taste rose into his mouth, almost choking him. He'd never been one to hope, but he sought it out now. Lucy had been the one thing he'd believed in.

"She's mine, isn't she?" His eyes bore into her, creating small holes. "Don't lie to me, Lucy. Is Elena my daughter?"

Lucy turned away. It wasn't the accusation in his eyes, it was the hurt she saw that was impossible to bear. "Yes."

Stunned, Dylan got out of bed, away from the woman he only thought he knew.

"I always believed that no matter what, the one thing I could rely on was that you'd always tell me the truth." Anger rumbled in his voice as he yanked on his jeans. "Dammit, Lucy, if Elena's mine, why didn't you tell me?" he demanded hotly. It was all he could do to keep from shaking the answer from her. "It wasn't like I didn't ask you."

The accusatory tone had her on her feet in an instant, with the bed between them like a barrier. "Because I didn't want you to think of her as a weapon, as a bargaining chip, that's why," she spat out hotly.

"What the hell are you talking about?"

Was he that thick, that blind? "I didn't want her to be the reason you came back to me—*if* you came back to me," she amended, knowing she had just made a giant leap. "I didn't want you to think I was trying to trap you."

He couldn't believe what she was saying. All this time, she'd carried his child within her, and she hadn't told him. Had actively kept the information from him. Was everything he'd believed about her a lie as well?

"So you lied to me?"

She felt trapped, her back against the wall. This wasn't coming out right at all. She wanted to have chosen her time, her place. Above all, she wanted him to understand why she had done it. But words eluded her, evaporating from her brain like so many beads of water in the sun. "It seemed like the thing to do at the time."

He rounded the bed, looming over her. "And at what time did you plan to tell me she was mine?"

Another lie would only make things worse. But the truth made nothing better. "I hadn't worked that out yet."

Because he was afraid of what he would do to her, he shoved his hands deep into his pockets. He grappled instead with his anger. And his hurt.

How could she?

"I believed you. When you told me she wasn't mine, I believed you. Believed you because I knew you'd never lie to me. Believed you even when it ripped out my insides to think that you could go to someone else's bed before the sheets we'd shared were even cool." Anger turned to rage, threatening to boil over. "Do you know what that did to me?"

The look in his eyes was frightening, but she wasn't going to allow it to intimidate her. She'd had things to struggle with herself. Things he'd probably never even considered.

Lucy tossed her hair over her shoulders, her eyes narrowing into angry slits. "About the same thing it did to me to have you leave without even a decent explanation."

Oh, no, she wasn't going to turn this around on him. She was the guilty one here. He'd done what he had to protect her. "So you did what?" he shouted at her. "You withheld the fact that Elena was my daughter from me just to punish me?"

She drew herself up. "If that's what you think, you never knew me at all."

He struggled to ignore the wounded look in her eyes. She wasn't going to distract him like that. He was the injured party here, not her. "If I hadn't come back when I did, you wouldn't have ever told me about my daughter, would you?"

He was whitewashing it, making her the heavy, she thought angrily.

"You didn't 'come back,'" she reminded him, her voice as infused with suppressed anger as his. "You were here on police business, to tell me my brother had been killed. If it hadn't been for that, for your damn case, you wouldn't be here now.''

The words cut deep. He was here to protect her, not because he wanted to solve the case. ''Is that what you think?''

Yes, that's what she thought. She didn't want to, but he'd given her no choice. She raised her chin pugnaciously. ''Am I wrong?''

The urge to throttle her was almost overwhelming. He couldn't risk remaining in the room with her much longer. ''I can't talk to you when you're like this.''

''You can't talk at all.'' She heard the baby begin to cry again. ''Now, if you'll excuse me, our daughter is crying.''

Turning on her heel, she walked out.

He watched her go.

Dylan raked his fingers through his hair, still fighting for composure as he drove to the stakeout. Anger choked him. Anger and a sense of betrayal the magnitude of which he'd never experienced before. Over the years, he'd come to expect nothing from no one. That way, he was never disappointed.

But he'd expected better from Lucy. She'd been different, so different from everyone else who had and did populate his life. And because she was different, she'd managed to slip through the barriers that were erected all around him and gotten inside.

He'd given Lucy the power to hurt him and now she had.

Because he couldn't safely predict what he'd do or say, he'd taken himself out of the volatile equation and left the house without another word.

Left, he realized belatedly now, without thinking. Argument or not, Lucy still needed someone to go with her and Elena to work. Or at least make sure she got off all right.

Reaching for his cell phone, Dylan swore at himself. What kind of a cop was he, anyway? He'd broken the first cardinal rule. He'd allowed his personal emotions to get in the way of his being a cop.

His finger poised to hit the buttons, he couldn't remember O'Hara's cell number. Exasperated, he tossed aside the cell phone and called dispatch instead, using the car phone.

"This is Detective McMorrow." He rattled off his badge number to verify his claim. "I need Detective O'Hara's cell number."

The woman on the other end gave it to him, then added, "But I don't think it's going to do you much good right now."

Impatience drummed lanky fingers through him. Now what? "Why?"

"Detective O'Hara just called in to say he was taking some personal time and would be gone the rest of the day. His wife just went into labor. He asked me to call you and tell you that he was sorry." It was clear from her tone that she had no idea why an apology was necessary. "But I couldn't reach you. Was your cell phone off?"

She asked the question out of thin air.

A single thought played and replayed itself through his mind. Lucy was alone. He'd left her alone. And there was no telling what she could be up against.

Gripping the wheel, one eye on the rearview mirror for any oncoming traffic, Dylan made a sharp U-turn in the middle of the block.

The car behind him came to a screeching halt, pulling onto the sidewalk. Dylan drove on without a backward glance.

She'd heard the front door slam and knew that he was gone. All the hot words that she had flung at him burned now on her tongue like acid. More than anything, she wanted to run after Dylan to demand to know what gave him the right to jerk her soul around this way.

She wanted him to hold her and apologize for what he'd said.

She wanted to apologize for what she'd said.

But she remained where she was, holding her daughter to her, forbidding herself to cry. Tears were for women who had lost something. You couldn't lose what you'd never had in the first place.

"But at least I have you," she whispered to the small face that looked up at her. Her heart aching, she kissed Elena's forehead. "And you are the very best part of both of us."

Lucy had just finished feeding Elena and placed the baby back into her crib when she heard the doorbell. Her heart began to race immediately.

"Is that your daddy? Did he come back to say he was sorry?" She wiped away traces of tears that had refused not to fall with the heel of her hand. "Probably not. Probably just somebody selling magazines."

Dylan wouldn't have rung the doorbell, he would have used his key, wouldn't he?

She no longer knew anything for sure as she hurried to the front door.

Maybe he was being formal. Distant. That would be just like him, she thought.

Reaching the front door, Lucy tightened the sash at her waist and braced herself for whatever was to come.

Or so she thought.

Dylan narrowly avoided merging with a silver Honda as he swerved around the vehicle, trying to make up for lost time. He was driving like a man with the devil on his tail, all the while telling himself he was behaving irrationally. There was no real reason to suspect that Lucy and Elena were in any sort of immediate danger. Just because there was no one to watch the house didn't automatically mean that someone had gotten to her.

"What're the odds, McMorrow? You're letting this whole case get to you," he upbraided himself, whizzing through a light that had just turned red.

But he couldn't shake the feeling. The feeling that he was right. That she and the baby *were* in danger. Palmero's men could have been watching the house all along. Watching the police watch her. And now the break in the link had come.

Dammit, why hadn't he noticed that the car parked across the street wasn't a Camry but another mid-size vehicle? Only the color had registered, and the color had been the same as O'Hara's vehicle. Navy blue.

He didn't waste time wondering if it was a coincidence or a plant left there on purpose so his attention wouldn't be drawn to the absence of a car.

All he could think about, all he could focus on, was getting back to Lucy before it was too late.

Lucy tried to shut the door, but she was no match for the two men who pushed their way into her house. Where was the man who was supposed to be guarding her? Why had he let Palmero and some man who looked like he was more suited to living his life in the world's dark shadows get by?

Praying that the detective was even now on the line calling for back up, she took a step away from the two. Despite the small hope she was trying to nurture, she was acutely aware that she was alone in the house with these two men.

Palmero looked at her with a cold, detached smile that didn't begin to reach his eyes. She had a feeling that he thrived on fear. She did her best to hide hers.

Steely gray-blue eyes washed over her, taking measure. "Really, Lucy, I am hurt. You don't return my calls, you turn down my generous offers to help you. You even snub my invitations." He placed his hand over his heart, the rings on his fingers glinting and winking at her, flirting with the sunlight coming through the windows. "Is that any way for a lovely woman in distress to behave?"

She didn't know who posed more of a threat, the man who was talking, or the one who wasn't. The latter was to the left of her, and she had an uneasy feeling he was about to circle behind her.

Still, she raised her chin, her eyes defiantly on Palmero's. "I'm not in distress."

"You think not?"

Palmero's smile bordered on malevolent, making

her blood run cold. All she could think of was Elena in the next room. They seemed to have forgotten about her. She prayed that the baby wouldn't cry and bring attention to herself.

"Why should I be in distress?"

Traces of the smile vanished as if it had never existed. "Because ladies who keep things that don't belong to them are always in distress." With his eyes, he motioned to the other man, who took a step closer to Lucy. She knew it was calculated to play on her fear, but that didn't stop the fear from growing. "I've been more than patient, but my patience is just about used up. I assure you, you don't want to be around when it is. Now, where is it?"

Dammit, why couldn't Ritchie just have worked for her full-time? Why had he gotten himself involved with this monster? "Where's what?"

"Don't act stupid, it doesn't become you." There was an edge to the smooth voice that drove her fear up another notch. "I like family loyalty. There isn't enough of it around these days." Palmero's eyes pinned her like a moth to a posterboard mount. "I hear you and your brother were very close, he shared everything with you."

Lucy backed away until she couldn't move any farther. The sofa was at her back, the coffee table and Palmero in front. "Not everything."

All pretense at patience dissolved. "The tape," he shouted into her face. "Where is the damn tape he took?"

"What tape?" she shouted back, her fear suddenly swallowed by anger at the threat this man posed to her daughter, by the cold realization that she was really facing the man who'd had her brother murdered. Adrenaline pushed aside common sense, giving her strength. "You've torn apart my house and my shop. If I had the damn tape, where could I have hidden it?"

"Exactly what I want to know."

Everything went still, underscoring the clink of the gun he was suddenly pointing at her.

She had one chance.

With a shriek meant to throw them off by just a fraction, Lucy ducked and shoved the coffee table straight at him, striking him squarely in the shins.

The gun went off, the shot going wild. A guttural cry came from the henchman at almost the same time. The man went down, clutching his shoulder and cursing as blood spilled through his spread fingers.

Enraged, Palmero jumped over the table and caught Lucy by the robe as she tried to get away. He yanked her to him so hard, the air was almost knocked out of her. The last remnants of Palmero's facade dropped away.

"You little bitch," he snarled into her face, the gun barrel pressed against her temple, "you're going to make this damned difficult, aren't you."

Holding her by the waist, he managed to pin both of her arms to her side. The metal felt cold against her skin as he ran it along the edge where the robe met her breasts. The sickening sweetness was back in his voice.

"Now, why do you want to do that when I can make this so pleasant for you?"

"Hey, I'm bleeding here, dammit," the man on the floor cried.

"Shut up, you've gotten worse shaving." Palmero's attention never left Lucy. "Now, talk."

It was all she could do not to tremble outwardly. Inside, she was vibrating. This had to have been the way Ritchie had felt in his last moments, she thought. Digging deep inside herself, Lucy played it the way she knew her brother would have. With bravado and sarcasm to the end, stalling and hoping for a last-minute miracle.

"Fine." Her voice was flippant. "What'll we talk about?"

"How about that he's going to let you go and then maybe I'll let him walk away with his life."

Lucy's heart lodged in her throat. The last-minute miracle she'd been praying for had materialized.

Dylan was in the doorway with his gun trained on Palmero.

Tightening his hold, Palmero raised his gun back to Lucy's temple. "Go ahead, shoot," he taunted. "You'll get her. And even if you don't, you think your bullet will reach me before mine reaches her brain?" He cocked the trigger. "I don't think so."

Dylan felt as if his own heart had stopped beating. One tiny miscalculation on his part and Lucy would pay for it with her life. But he had to play it from a position of strength. Men like Palmero understood nothing else.

His eyes never left the other man's face. Dylan's voice was calm, as if he was ordering a bland breakfast special from a worn menu. "Put it down, Palmero. You're still alive, we can work things out. The police are on their way, you've got nothing to gain by killing her."

Palmero's smile widened, appearing almost maniacal. "Does the word *satisfaction* mean anything to you?" He moved the barrel slowly along Lucy's forehead, bringing it back to its original position. His eyes dared Dylan to make a move.

Dylan had no choice. The man could kill as easily as he could draw breath. He could see it in his eyes. Dylan let his weapon fall laxly in his hands, spreading his thumb and three fingers wide around it. It dangled from the remaining finger.

"All right, I'm putting it down." Dylan bent his knees, sinking down slowly and watching Palmero. "Let her go." He set the weapon on the floor in front of him.

Keen on his victory, Palmero cocked his head, smirking. "You disappoint me, McMorrow. I thought it would be more of a contest between us. You know, guns blazing, damsel in distress bleeding as she sank to the ground, that sort of thing."

The look in Dylan's eyes damned the man's soul to hell. He kept his hands raised. "Maybe next time."

A look of solemnity came over Palmero's face as he took careful aim at Dylan. "There isn't going to be a next time."

Terror filled Lucy. He was going to kill Dylan. With all her might, Lucy swung her leg back and dug her heel into Palmero's shin, hitting the same spot that she'd gotten before with the table.

Caught by surprise, Palmero yelped, his hold on her waist loosening. Lucy twisted around and tried to grab the gun out of his hand. It discharged.

The next moment, Dylan was holding the gun he'd just laid down in his hand, aiming it at Palmero. The air turned blue around him as the other man cursed at both of them in frustration.

"Daniels, get up," Palmero shrieked at his man, but the latter had lost too much blood to rise to his feet on his own.

Dylan stretched his free arm out to Lucy. Stifling a sob, Lucy fell into it.

It was then that she saw the blood on the front of his shirt.

She stared at it in horror, then looked up at him. "You're hurt."

He was having trouble breathing and it was hard to keep his head from spinning. The distant sound of sirens was breaking apart the morning air. He had to hang on until they arrived.

"Just a scratch," he murmured. Palmero looked to the rear of the house. Dylan read his intent. "Here." He shoved the gun handle toward Lucy. "Hold it on him. Shoot him if he tries anything. They're almost here."

Her hand tightened around the weapon. It felt so unfamiliar to her. She'd only been on the firing range once in her life. Ritchie had made her go. She couldn't hit anything or even come close.

Dylan sank to his knees beside her, terrifying her. She knew he was struggling to remain conscious. It took all she could do not to take him in her arms and hold him, but she couldn't afford to. Lucy saw the look on Palmero's face. He was going to make a break for it. It was his only chance.

She steadied the weapon with her other hand and smiled, thinking of the old line she'd always liked. She pulled back the trigger, her eyes on Palmero. "Go ahead, just give me an excuse. Make my day."

She heard Dylan laugh softly, the sound almost faint. "That's my girl."

Chapter 16

Lucy felt like her head was spinning. Everything had happened so quickly in the last half hour, and now she was standing out here in the hospital corridor, watching the lights play off the pastel-colored walls, while Elena slept in her infant seat on the floor right beside her leg.

She didn't know how much more of this waiting she could take. Why didn't someone come out and talk to her, tell her how Dylan was doing?

Waiting was making her crazy.

There were things she wanted to say to Dylan, things that had occurred to her only after she had ridden in the ambulance with him and after the paramedics had taken him from her. Even after she'd stood, watching the surgery room doors close, leaving him on the inside and her on the outside.

So many things. Private things, like she loved him and she was determined to remain in his life on whatever terms they could work out together. Public things, like the call she'd just gotten from Alma on the cell phone she'd almost forgotten to take with her. She'd grabbed it at the last minute, just before they had all rushed out of the house. Dylan went in an ambulance to one hospital while Daniels, the other wounded man, was taken to another.

Lucy had taken all of three minutes to throw on some clothes and grab a couple of things for Elena. Dylan had lost consciousness and there was a bullet lodged in the vicinity of his heart. Scared, she had no idea how close she was to losing everything. There was absolutely no way she was going to remain behind while they took him to the hospital.

Restless, she was about to pick Elena up and begin pacing when she saw a broad-chested man hurrying toward her. Their eyes met. There was a question in his.

"Lucy?" She nodded and he put out his hand. "I'm Dave Watley, Dylan's partner." The captain had called him, filling him in on the details and telling him to close up shop. It looked like they had their man after all.

From everything Dylan had told him and everything he hadn't, Watley had a feeling he would find Lucy Alvarez here. He nodded toward the double doors. "How's he doing?"

It was the same question that had been ricocheting through Lucy's brain now for the last hour. Feeling helpless, she shook her head. "I don't know. I can't get anyone to tell me. He's been in surgery since they brought him in."

Watley saw the anguish in her eyes. Everything

about her body language declared Lucy to be a woman tottering on the edge of exasperation and despair. Looked like, stumbling blindly in the dark, Dylan had gotten himself a keeper, he thought.

He slipped a comforting arm around her shoulders. "McMorrow's a tough son of a gun. This isn't the first bullet he's caught. He'll pull through."

"I know," she murmured, but she knew nothing of the sort. Her eyes were bright with tears when she looked at Watley. "He has to. So I can tell him his case is solved."

Watley looked at her in surprise. "You know Palmero's man rolled on him?"

"What?"

Obviously, she didn't, so Watley told her. "Daniels thought he was going to die. Turns out he's the religious sort and was afraid of meeting his Maker with a bad conscience. They took him to Mercy General. The guy talked all the way. Nonstop confession. Luckily the cop was there to read him his rights," Watley said, laughing dryly. "We should have leaned on Daniels to begin with." He could see by her expression that they were not talking about the same thing, at least not completely. "Why did you think the case was solved?"

Elena was beginning to stir. Bending down, Lucy picked the baby up. "A package came to the shop in this morning's mail marked Return to Sender. It was undeliverable because there was postage due. The handwriting on it was Ritchie's."

"Was it the tape?" Watley asked. They had found out from Daniels that Ritchie had stolen one of the restaurant's surveillance tapes, the one that showed Michelson being murdered. Daniels said he'd tried to blackmail Palmero with it.

She nodded. "I had Alma open the package." Even now, it was hard for her to believe that this had all happened because of something on a videotape. As soon as he was better, she was going to make Dylan tell her everything.

"She have it now?"

Lucy nodded, rubbing Elena's back to soothe the baby back to sleep. "I just called your captain. He sent someone to get it."

"Good thinking. Who was your brother mailing the tape to?"

"Me, at the house." One way or another, Ritchie had intended to wind up with the tape.

"Lucky thing he didn't put enough postage on it. That kept it out of circulation for several weeks," Watley remarked.

"Yes, lucky," she echoed.

But she knew that luck didn't have anything to do with it. They had a postage machine in the storeroom. Ritchie had used it countless times. He'd mailed the package out with insufficient postage on purpose. Just in case Palmero's men came looking for the tape at the house and the shop. He knew from experience that the tape would be out of circulation for up to a month, if not more.

She was too drained to explain anything to the man beside her.

The door opened behind her and she sprang to attention, cornering the doctor who came out. "How is he?"

The man undid the surgical mask he was wearing, letting it hang at half-mast around his neck.

"Hard to hold down," the physician commented with a wry smile. "Are you Lucy?"

"Yes," she breathed, trying to read his expression, praying that the news wasn't bad.

The doctor gestured to his right. Dylan had been transferred from the operating room to another area via a back route. "He's asking for you. Room 112."

Eager to see him, Lucy still hesitated, looking at Elena. Her dilemma was clear.

Watley stepped in. "Don't give her another thought. I can watch your daughter until you come out." His smile was reassuring. "It'll be good practice for me. We're having our first pretty soon now."

Rather than saying anything, she kissed his cheek and hurried down the hall to the room the doctor pointed out to her. Suddenly nervous, she took a deep breath before slipping inside.

Dylan looked as if he was asleep. She could feel her nerves twisting around her heart and squeezing. There were bandages crisscrossed over his chest, looping over his left shoulder. His left arm was bandaged all the way down to his elbow.

When she thought of how close he had come to being killed...

She saw his eyes flutter and then open, looking at her. Relief flooded her, threatening to steal her breath. It took a second for her to find her voice. "I hear you're giving everyone a hard time."

Dylan tried to sit up. She crossed to the bed quickly, wanting to push him back, afraid to touch him and cause him any more pain than he already had.

Concern had etched deep lines into his face. "Are you all right?"

No, she wasn't all right. She'd been to hell and back in the space of an hour. But she lifted a careless shoulder, letting it drop. "I wasn't the one who was shot," she reminded him. She wasn't going to make a fool of herself and cry, she warned herself. But she felt her eyes smarting. "The question is, how are you?"

A sound escaped his lips that sounded suspiciously like a deprecating laugh. "I'll live."

"Nice to know." She tried her best to sound flippant, thinking she wasn't pulling it off too well. He had scared the hell out of her when he had passed out at her feet. She'd been so afraid that the wound was fatal. "According to your partner, so will Palmero's lackey. Long enough to roll over on him."

She could see his mind working as it focused on what she was saying. That was when he was most alive, she thought, when he was concentrating on his work. Not on his personal life. Not on her. It was something she was going to have to come to terms with if she wanted to make a place for herself in his life.

She was more than willing to try. The last hour had shown her that.

"So he talked?" Dylan finally managed to say. Did she know how relieved he was to open his eyes and see her here? Did she have any idea what he had gone through, driving back to her house, terrified that something had happened to her?

She nodded. "Nonstop, Watley says. And the tape turned up."

With his good arm, he pushed himself up on the bed. "Where?"

"At the shop," she answered glibly. "Ritchie mailed it from there to me—at the house. With just enough postage to keep it from being delivered. It was lying in the post office the whole time Palmero's people were ransacking my place."

Dylan shook his head in admiration. "Ritchie always was sharp."

That was his take on it, she thought. She pressed her lips together grimly. "Maybe if he'd been a little less sharp, he'd still be around."

He agreed with her but was at a loss what to say in response. "Where's Elena?"

Lucy indicated the door and the corridor beyond. "Your partner's watching her. Said it would be good practice for him." Dylan's face looked drawn, tired and so pale. How much blood had he lost? "Looks like you won't have to be guarding me any longer."

Dylan looked at her, trying to gauge her tone. Was she happy about that? Relieved that she was out of danger, or relieved that he was going to be out of her life? He couldn't tell. "Looks like."

When he made no effort to add anything further to that, she stared at him. Schooling herself for a break still didn't help her when she was faced with it. Dammit, she'd nearly died out there, waiting to hear whether or not he was going to pull through, and now he was just shrugging her off like this?

"So that's it?" she demanded hotly. "You play the big heroic scene and then you move on out of my life again?"

He didn't understand what she was getting so

angry about. He thought she wanted him to go. "Is that what *you* want?"

Hands on her hips, she faced him squarely, fire in her eyes. "Is that what *you* want?"

He thought that he had never seen anyone so magnificent in his life. "I asked first."

She could have choked him then. "Don't play etiquette games with me, McMorrow. I want an answer, dammit. Are you planning on drifting through my life every ten months or so, making love with me and then disappearing off the face of the earth? Is that the kind of life you want?"

More than anything in the world, he wanted to kiss her. But even more than that, he wanted to spare her. "No, but it might be better for you in the long run."

Where the hell did he get off, telling her what was better for her? "Don't you think I should be the one to make that decision instead of having it made for me?"

It took everything he had not to beg her to stay. Beg her to remain despite everything. But it wouldn't be fair to her. "You can't make a decision unless you have all the facts."

She had no idea what he was talking about, only that there were still secrets between them and she hated that, hated that he kept things from her. "So tell me, tell me all the facts, Dylan." *Tell me you love me, Dylan.*

Where did he start? And how? How did he tell her about his life? This had been so much a part of him for so long, it seemed to have no beginning. It had just always been.

But he knew he had to try. If there was ever

going to be a tomorrow, he had to try. And even if
she turned her back on him and walked away after
she heard, he owed Lucy an explanation because of
the child they had created together.

"Did you know that kids who are abused tend to
grow up and become abusers? And that boys who
grow up in homes seeing their mother beaten by
their father tend to perpetuate the same behavior
when they get married? They beat their own
wives."

Slowly, the shroud was beginning to lift for her.
"Are you telling me that you were abused as a
child? That your mother was abused?" Was that
what he was afraid of? That he would treat her the
way his father had treated his mother? Didn't he
know any better than that?

"Abused," Dylan echoed. "Such a clean, sani-
tary word for what went on in that house." He
hated remembering, had done everything he could
to block the memories. But for her sake, he dug
them out one more time and brought them into the
light of day. "My father was like a walking time
bomb, except you never knew what his settings
were. He could go off at the slightest thing, anytime. Christmas, birthdays, riding in the car, it
didn't matter where, didn't matter when. Somebody
said something and suddenly he was this raging maniac, punching, beating, cursing. It was almost always aimed at my mother." It only included him
when he got in the way. When he tried to save his
mother. Or when his father was trying to teach his
mother a lesson.

He looked at Lucy, an ironic, sad smile on his
lips. "And she took it. For twenty-six years, my

mother took it. Until she couldn't take it anymore and died.''

''He killed her?'' she asked in horror.

He shook his head. ''Not directly. But he's responsible all the same. She died because she couldn't bring herself to walk away and hurt him. That's what she told me, she didn't want to hurt him. Never mind how many times he actually physically hurt her.''

''What does this have to do with us?''

''Weren't you listening?'' he demanded heatedly. ''The children of wife beaters beat their own wives. Abused kids grow up to abuse their own kids.''

He was throwing statistics at her. She was looking at a man, not a statistic. A man she loved. A man she knew. ''Not every time.''

She was too good, too pure, too optimistic. She didn't know anything of the world he knew. ''Enough to make it count. Enough to make it a threat.''

He couldn't just turn his back on what they had because he was afraid of what could happen. She wouldn't let him. Beside him now, she placed her hand on his, willing him to look at her. To believe her.

''You said I wasn't listening. Maybe I wasn't. But I was seeing. And remembering. Remembering what you were like, holding Elena. How angry you were when you realized I had intended to keep you out of her life.'' Her eyes softened. ''And remembering how you were with me.'' She brought her face in close to his. ''The only way you could hurt me is by walking out again, the way you did last time.''

He wanted to believe what she believed. But he remembered the promises his father made to his mother. Tears streaming down his face, begging her forgiveness and swearing he would never raise a hand to her again. Until the next time. ''You don't know what you're saying. This is for your own good.''

''Let me be the judge of what's for my own good.'' Her eyes held his. ''And I pick you. You're for my own good, Dylan. My own good and Elena's.''

He had never known what love really was. That it could feel like this. Like sunshine struggling to fill him, to take over every part of him. She was his love, and his sunshine.

''You might live to regret this.''

''Not a chance.'' She took a step back. Watley was still outside with Elena. Maybe she should get back to him. ''Get some rest, I'll be back to see you in the morning.''

But he held out his hand to her, drawing her back with the look in his eyes.

''Lucy, don't leave yet.'' Funny, he'd faced down the bore of Palmero's gun with far less nervousness than he felt traveling through him now. ''I want to say something to you.''

''I think you've already said more to me just now than you have the entire time we've known each other,'' she teased. But she moved back to the bed despite her words. ''Go ahead, I'm listening.''

He wanted to phrase this just right, but words

were beginning to scatter through his mind like so many pinballs after the plunger had struck them.

"When I suddenly realized that I'd walked off and left you without checking on O'Hara—"

He was going to apologize for putting her in harm's way. There was no need to go over all that. "You were angry."

He waved away her words, wishing she'd let him get this out before he lost his nerve. Damn, she deserved candlelight and soft music, not the glaring whiteness of a hospital room. "That's no excuse. My being angry could have cost you your life."

"But it didn't, and that's what counts. You can't go through life speculating about what might have happened, thinking about the worst possibilities. That's—"

He caught her hand, stopping her before she could get wound up. "Can I finish?"

She grinned, inclining her head. "Okay."

"I realized at that moment that I didn't want to live in a world that didn't have you in it." He saw the smile fade from her lips as she stared at him incredulously. Was he making a terrible mess of it? he wondered as he pushed on. "That I couldn't live in it. And I realized that if you weren't around, there'd be no reason for me to go on." He paused, fumbling. "Help me out here."

And then the smile returned as she shook her head. "Nope. You're doing fine on your own."

With one hand, he was at a disadvantage. All he could do was hold hers with it. "That's just it, I'm not. I haven't been for a long time." He thought that over. "Maybe never. I don't want to be alone anymore. Loving you has changed everything."

"Loving me?" she echoed, stunned. She'd been hoping for some word of affection. To have him utter the final pronouncement was far beyond what she thought she would ever hear. "You love me?"

"I love you."

Speechless, she forced each word out individually. "When did this happen?"

"I'm not sure. It kind of snuck in early on when I wasn't looking. But I'm looking now and I want to go on looking at you—and Elena—for the rest of my life. Marry me, Lucy. Elena needs a father—and I need you. More than anything else in the world, I need you." What she had said was right, he realized. He knew it now, in his soul, a soul he only had because of her. "I don't have to turn into my father. I haven't up to now."

"And you won't." She cupped her hand to his cheek, so full of love she didn't know how it didn't just come pouring out of her. "There's a kind, caring man inside there behind those bars you put up. He just needs a little coaxing to come out."

He ran his hand along her shoulder, his eyes teasing hers. "You up to coaxing?"

"I think so." Her mouth curved mischievously. "You know, I'm not wearing anything under this. I just threw these on so I could go with you in the ambulance."

His eyes indicated the curtain that hung from the ceiling and ran along the perimeter of his bed. "Why don't you pull that closed?" he suggested.

She did as he asked, then came back to him. He took her hand, drawing her to him.

She hesitated, concerned about his condition. "What about your shoulder?"

Dylan feathered his fingers through her hair, cupping her cheek. Silently pledging his life and his soul to her with his eyes.

"Right now, my shoulder is the furthest thing from my mind."

And as he kissed her, she believed him.

* * * * *

Look for Marie Ferrarrella's next book,

THOSE MATCHMAKING BABIES,

*on sale in August, available
from Silhouette Romance.*

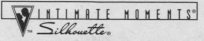

presents a riveting 12-book continuity series:

A YEAR OF LOVING DANGEROUSLY

When dishonor threatens a top-secret agency, twelve
of the best agents in the world are determined to uncover a
deadly traitor in their midst. These brave men and women
are prepared to risk it all as they put their lives—
and their hearts—on the line.

Be there from the very beginning....

MISSION: IRRESISTIBLE by Sharon Sala
(July 2000)

She was there to catch a traitor, and getting passionately
involved with stubborn, sexy East Kirby was *not* an option for
Alicia Corbin. But then she discovered that the brooding
operative—whom she'd been instructed to bring back to the
field—was the soul mate she'd been searching for. Now if only
she could make her mission a success—and East a partner for life!

A YEAR OF LOVING DANGEROUSLY:
Where passion rules and nothing is what is seems....

*Available only from Silhouette Intimate Moments
at your favorite retail outlet.*

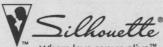

Where love comes alive™

Look Who's Celebrating Our 20th Anniversary:

"In 1980, Silhouette gave a home to my first book and became my family. Happy 20th Anniversary! And may we celebrate twenty more."

—*New York Times* bestselling author
Nora Roberts

"Twenty years of Silhouette! I can hardly believe it. Looking back on it, I find that my life and my books for Silhouette were inextricably intertwined.... Every Silhouette I wrote was a piece of my life. So, thank you, Silhouette, and may you have many more anniversaries."

—International bestselling author
Candace Camp

"Twenty years publishing fiction by women, for women, and about women is something to celebrate! I am honored to be a part of Silhouette's proud tradition— one that I have no doubt will continue being cherished by women the world over for a long, long time to come."

—International bestselling author
Maggie Shayne

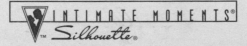

INTIMATE MOMENTS®
Silhouette®